CRAZY FOR THE BEST MAN

CRAZY IN LOVE #2

ASHLEE MALLORY

ISBN: 978-0-9970035-3-6 (E-Book)

ISBN: 978-0-9970035-5-0 (Paperback)

Cover design: RBA Designs

Developmental Editor: CeCe Carroll

Copy/Line Editor: Blue Otter Editing

ALSO BY ASHLEE MALLORY

Sweet Contemporary Romance

Crazy in Love Series:

Crazy for the Boss

Crazy for the Best Man

Crazy for the Rock Star

Sorensen Family Series:

Her Backup Boyfriend

Her Accidental Husband

The Playboy's Proposal

Her Surprise Engagement

Romantic Suspense

You Again

Love You Madly

Thriller

Deceived

CHAPTER 1

IT WAS PROBABLY A COINCIDENCE.

Anna Blake's editor asking her to come in on what would normally be her work-from-home day might not have anything to do with the story that ran in this morning's *San Francisco Chronicle*. The foreboding that had her palms sweating and her right eye twitching, however, told her otherwise.

Anna stepped in front of the open door of the editor in chief at *The Daily Rundown*, Charlotte "Charlie" Kravitz, and peered in. The woman in question was staring at her computer screen, unaware of Anna's presence. Before she lost her nerve, Anna knocked on the door.

Charlie glanced up, not even attempting to crack a smile when she saw her. "Anna. Good. Please, come in and shut the door."

"Sure," Anna said, keeping her voice upbeat. Her hands full with two specialty coffee drinks she picked up at the coffee shop downstairs, she managed to shut the door and sit down in the chair across from her editor.

"I thought you might need this," Anna said, and placed

the double-shot espresso drink in front of Charlie, who, even though it was almost seventy degrees in downtown San Francisco on this unusually balmy June day, liked her coffee piping hot.

Anna was not above groveling as the occasion warranted.

Only Charlie didn't reach for the coffee. Instead, without preamble, she turned her computer screen around to face Anna, giving her a moment to peruse the screen. Anna barely glanced at it, the caption above the story already too familiar.

Yep. Today's meeting was definitely not a coincidence.

"Captivating stuff," Charlie drawled after another long minute. Anna looked up to find the woman studying her with those cool green eyes, a stark contrast to her red spiky hair that was always wild and disheveled. "Who knew that, when Malcolm Van Hollins kicked the bucket three months ago, his last will and testament would make such a shocking revelation. Imagine, another heir, another daughter that no one had heard about until now. At least *I* hadn't heard about her, despite the fact I've had the Van Hollins family on my top ten most wanted news lead list since—well, since young Janie's first Instagram photo went viral six years ago. You are familiar with the list, aren't you?"

Okay, that had to be more rhetorical, since the top ten list in question was written and hanging on the wall behind Charlie. "Yes, Charlie," Anna said, just in case an answer was necessary.

Charlie reached across her desk and pulled the coffee to her, removing the lid and stirring it with the end of a pen she had on her desk as she continued. "Do you also remember that day last fall when Janie announced her engagement to Dax St. Claire, youngest son of the late US

Senator Thomas St. Claire, and I pointedly dropped the Van Hollins name from number eight to"—the woman looked back at the board, as if she couldn't remember where the Van Hollinses fell on the list—"number three? You do? Good. Well, imagine my surprise this morning when my Google alerts notified me of this hot new scoop involving the Van Hollinses' lost heir, who not only do I know but who also happens to be one of my very own staff writers here at *The Rundown*. And this lucky girl was not only going to be a guest at the upcoming exclusive five-day wedding event of the year but was also a bridesmaid according to Miss Janie Van Hollins herself."

"Now that is completely untrue," Anna said, finally finding something to latch on to. "I never told Janie I was going, let alone that I was going to be a bridesmaid."

And why would she? Her biological father had pretended she didn't exist her entire life. He'd never called, never sent her presents for her birthday or for the holidays, not even a lousy card. Anna used to muse that, if she met him on the street, he probably wouldn't know who she was.

Despite Malcolm Van Hollins's lack of interest in anything to do with his eldest daughter, the man wasn't so averse to making room in his life for his other daughter. The girl who was the apple of her father's eye, at least according to the article Anna read when she was fourteen.

"I see. You disagree with the part about your participation in the wedding, but the rest... it's accurate?" Charlie asked. "You are Malcolm Van Hollins's daughter."

There was no use trying to escape it. Anna sighed. "Unfortunately, yes, but since the man ignored my existence for the past twenty-eight years, it's not something I ordinarily like to talk about. Let alone share for the sake of gossip to potentially thousands of online readers."

Anna would have gladly kept the news of her father's identity hidden the rest of her life, and likely would have, had Malcolm not succumbed to his massive stroke in April, leaving her a sizable inheritance, wanted or not.

To Anna, the money felt almost...tainted. Like it was either Malcolm's lame attempt at an apology for never being part of her life or, worse, hush money. Needless to say, Anna hadn't touched it, nor did she intend on ever spending a dime of it, even if the money would make her life easier in ways she'd never before experienced. Instead, she was researching the right charity where she hoped to donate the entirety of the money by Christmas.

Charlie took a sip of her drink. "I won't pretend to understand what you're going through, but I will say that I'm terribly disappointed that you let your personal bias cloud your judgment as a reporter. Do you remember when you first came to me two years ago, promising me that you would go above and beyond every other reporter here if I would only give you a chance to write for me?"

"Of course, Charlie." Anna also remembered how she had shown Charlie dozens of human-interest news stories that she'd previously written for several other online journals, but Charlie hadn't even looked at them. Instead, she'd said she'd give her a shot, start her off in the magazine's entertainment news section and see how she did. Unfortunately—or fortunately, depending how you looked at it—Anna had a talent for getting the latest gossip scoops first, and two years later, she was still in the position because she was too valuable to be anywhere else.

And so Anna's career had been sidelined for dishing on the latest who's-dating-whom Hollywood gossip, who wore what designer to what big red-carpet affair, and who was rumored to be stepping out on his pregnant wife.

"Then you might understand why, after everything you promised, I feel cheated by"—Charlie waved to the computer screen—"this, and all the hits this story is generating for the *Chronicle* that should have been ours."

"I'm sorry, Charlie. I...I underestimated people's interest in this." Okay, so maybe that wasn't exactly true, but Anna's job was reporting news and gossip about other people's lives, not her own.

Charlie grabbed her glasses from the desk and put them on her face, giving the appearance of a disapproving schoolmarm. "That's where your personal stake in this has clouded your judgment and why you should have come to me, let me be the judge of what's print-worthy and what isn't. There is a reason the Van Hollins name is on that list. People want to know anything and everything about them, Janie Van Hollins in particular. The Van Hollins name has been a virtual institution in San Francisco society for years."

"You're right. It was a complete failure on my part, and I promise you that I'll come to you with anything in the future, regardless of my personal involvement."

Charlie's gaze turned speculative. "Fortunately for you, I think we can still salvage something from all of this."

Feeling like she was off of the proverbial hot seat, Anna shrugged and took a drink of her iced chai tea. "I don't know. The *Chronicle* story was pretty thorough. I don't think I could add anything more. It's not like I've ever met any of them."

"Of course it was thorough. I didn't mean adding anything more to *that* story. I'm talking about covering an entirely new one. Specifically, Janie Van Hollins's wedding, the wedding of the year that you will be going to in two weeks' time."

Anna's stomach roiled. "I don't think that's a good idea—"

Charlie held her hand up, cutting Anna off. "Save it. You have exclusive access to this wedding in all of its over-budgeted and over-the-top glory, and you're not going to waste it. You claim to be a reporter, and any good reporter would look at this as an opportunity to salvage the situation and come away with a more newsworthy story."

"You...you want me to dish the dirt on my fam—" She choked on the words before correcting herself. "The Van Hollinses?" She didn't exactly have any warm-fuzzy feelings toward any of them, but this seemed low. "I don't know if that's something I feel comfortable doing."

Charlie stared at her with that unblinking laser-like stare. "This isn't an option."

Anna blinked. "Wait. You mean, if I don't do this, you're going to...fire me?"

"Do you know how many emails and calls come into this office every day from new writers and more seasoned reporters than you who are interested in writing here? In the past two years, our online presence has increased one hundred and seventy-five percent and we're reaching more people than ever before. And every one of those reporters tells me the same thing: that they will do whatever they need to do to get the stories that people want to read. Kind of like what you once told me. And if you've had a change of heart, then why shouldn't I find someone who can get it done?"

Anna exhaled, trying to calm herself. She needed this job. Sure, it didn't pay all that much, but it was steady income that, when combined with the money her two room-mates added, paid the rent.

"These people," Charlie continued, indifferent to Anna's

rising panic, "the Van Hollinses, the St. Claires, and everyone else associated with those families and who will inevitably be in attendance at the wedding, they are what people want to read about. Maybe you can read the name placed in the number one spot behind me."

Anna didn't have to look to know the answer. The other half of the reason she was opposed to going to this nightmare of a wedding. "The St. Claires."

"That's right, and the fact that you're willing to waste the opportunity to cover this event, to get some dirt on these people, has me concerned."

She had a point. Anna was letting her personal hangups stop her from getting the inside scoop on possibly the most click-bait stories of the year, which was precisely the job Charlie had hired her to do. She didn't owe these people anything.

"You're absolutely right, Charlie, and I promise that I won't waste this opportunity. You'll have a great story," Anna said with absolute sincerity, even if it was going to require that she return the handful of calls that Janie had left over the past month. Calls that Anna had never had any intention of returning before now.

"That's what I thought," Charlie said, her mouth widening into as close to a smile as she was capable of. "You're tough, Anna, and with the right incentive, you can do anything. I mean, who knows how many family skeletons there are for you to discover? You'll be in the perfect position to ferret those out."

Was she really going to do this? Could she even do this? Talk to those people? Smile and pretend that it hadn't hurt that her own father had ignored her existence for her entire life?

Then there was the inevitability that she was going to

see *him* again. But that was something she wasn't ready to accept yet. One step at a time.

"I guess I had better reach out to Janie," Anna said and headed toward the door. "See if that offer's still good." After all, the wedding was only a couple weeks away, and it was possible that Janie could have found another bridesmaid, or worse, revoked the invitation.

"For your sake, let's hope it still is."

GOOD LORD. This was going to be a long week.

Nick St. Claire took the glass of whiskey the bartender poured him and strolled out to the courtyard of the Van Hollins estate in Napa, where tonight's informal gathering was taking place. The attendees were sparse since the bride had wanted to keep things intimate to give the members of the bridal party—such as the bridesmaids and groomsmen, the readers and ushers—a chance to get reacquainted.

The only problem was, with so few people, finding a nice out-of-the-way spot to chill and not invite attention was out of the question. A problem that became apparent when he spied Janie's bridesmaids already headed in his direction, one bridesmaid specifically whose gaze was set markedly on him. Sara DeWinters. Not just one of Janie's oldest friends but also a woman who Nick had made the mistake of getting entangled with last year and had who he'd been trying to get himself permanently disentangled from ever since.

The woman couldn't accept that things were over, a sentiment she shared with Nick's mother, Kathryn St. Claire, who, since the breakup, had been reminding him of all the reasons he and Sara had been a perfect match. Reasons like her family's political connections, not to mention their money and obvious social influence, all things that Kathryn esteemed above all others.

Nick wasn't ready for this, wasn't ready to have the complete and undivided attention of Janie's very young, very superficial, and very single friends. Not when he didn't have reinforcements from the other groomsmen to help allay their attention.

He turned his head, looking for any kind of distraction that would halt their approach. Where was Dax when he needed him? Probably off canoodling with his future bride, or maybe he'd decided to pick up the errant groomsman from the airport...

Wait a minute.

Nick's gaze fell on a blonde standing over at the bar, watching the bartender pour her a glass of wine. He was almost certain that he hadn't met her before. Last he'd heard, Janie's fourth bridesmaid and maid of honor was currently laid up in the hospital after a wakeboarding disaster and wasn't going to make it here at all.

Well, whoever the blonde was, she might be what he needed to hold off the three lemmings who were almost on him. Without a second to spare, Nick strode over, noticing the woman's long, shapely legs, legs that told him she earned her figure not by starving herself on kale smoothies and raw almonds but through actual sweat. As she turned around, he noticed a few of the woman's other attributes, like a pert nose, full, rosy lips, and clear, glowing skin.

Before he could second-guess his decision, Nick placed his hand on her arm, hoping that, should anyone be watching, they might assume they knew each other. Only, instead of mild surprise, the woman jumped a good inch at his touch before whirling to face him, her eyes blaring with fury.

Great. Add a well-deserved assault charge to what was sure to be a dreadful week.

"Excuse me," the blonde sputtered as he carefully placed himself between her and the bridesmaids' line of sight, attempting to minimize the damage of his ill-thought-out strategy.

"My apologies. I mistook you for...for someone else," he said lamely, adding a grin that usually had women flustered and eager to return his smile. Not so with this one. In fact, from the fire in those bluish-gray eyes, he was betting that an apology alone was not going to suffice.

He glanced over his shoulder, noticing with some relief that the trio had stopped their approach and were instead keeping a careful eye on him and the mystery woman.

Nick turned back to find the blonde staring at him, only now her anger had turned to something closer to horror and her eyes had widened as if in recognition. People's reactions when they realized who he was always varied to some degree. But he had to admit, this woman's shock was anything but the usual happy surprise or curiosity he received. No, her eyes narrowed to near slits and her face had taken on a splotchy red color.

There was a quick flash of something that hit him, a memory that niggled at him. There was something familiar about her...

He studied her again, trying to figure out why she reminded him of someone. Her long blonde hair was a mix of dark honey and golden strands as it flowed around her shoulders, and her face, angry splotchiness aside, had a slight sun-kissed tone, as if she tried to remember to wear sunblock but forgot half the time. Her eyes were a little wider-set than current beauty standards dictated, giving her a more distinctive quality, and compelled him to reach further back into his memory, to a time when he'd found satisfaction at drawing her ire.

She still hadn't spoken, although her mouth opened and closed as if she was struggling for words. He needed to try again. To dig for that natural St. Claire charm and put her at ease and assure her that he wasn't some pervert. Despite the anger that still reverberated in her tense shoulders and pursed lips, she was definitely someone he thought he might want to get reacquainted with, someone who might make these next few days less onerous.

"I'm Nick. Nick St. Claire. And you are?"

She still didn't respond, but her brows shot up and she gave him a look that seemed to tell him he shouldn't have to ask. Before he could question her further, however, a high-pitched squeal drew both their attention to the small blonde blur in pink who was racing in their direction.

"You're here!" Janie Van Hollins screamed before launching herself into the blonde's arms.

Nick's brother, Dax, followed his soon-to-be bride, a curious smile on his face as he watched the women's reunion. The blonde stood stiffly under Janie's embrace, quietly waiting for the tinier woman to disengage, which she eventually did with reluctance.

"To tell you the truth, I had some doubts that you were going to come," Janie said, staring in wonderment at the woman. "Not that I could blame you, under the circumstances. The fact that you still came, after everything"—Janie fanned her hand in front of her face as if to ward off tears—"well, it means more to me than you know."

"I'm happy that I was able to move some things around on my schedule to make it after all." The blonde attempted to smile back, but the smile didn't quite reach her eyes.

"Well, now that you're here, I want you to meet this

lovable, cuddly bear of mine," Janie said in that nauseating baby talk she employed so often when she talked about Dax. "This is the man who, in four more days, is going to be my husband, Dax St. Claire. And this is Dax's brother, Nick, our best man. Gentlemen, may I present my...my sister."

Sister. That explained their similarities, at least in physical appearance. Nick recalled Dax mentioning something about a family fury a month or so back when it came out that Malcolm Van Hollins had had a love child stashed away that no one knew about.

But that still didn't explain his sense of déjà vu. Was she a lobbyist? Had she been working on his rival's campaign? Or could she be a friend of his mother?

"Anna's a reporter for *The Daily Rundown*," Janie burst in proudly. "You may have seen her byline—that's the right word, isn't it? Anna Blake."

And in a flash, it all came back. Why he remembered this woman.

And why, if he had any sense, he'd take leave of everyone and run.

CHAPTER 2

THIS WAS TOO MUCH.

Anna had known the moment she agreed to come to this thing that she was going to have to confront the demons from her past. But having one such demon not remember her was too much. Especially after he'd made her junior year of high school a living hell. To be fair, she'd made his final year at Parrish Hall just as miserable, but it wasn't as if he hadn't had it coming to him.

From the look of shock and horror stamped on Nick's too-handsome face, it was all coming back to him. "Anna Blake." He nodded his head, his lips curling back in distaste. "What's it been? Ten years?"

"Give or take."

"More than enough time, I trust, for you to learn the value of verifying your sources."

Anna's right eye twitched involuntarily. *He's just trying to throw you off balance. Don't give him the satisfaction.*

She relaxed her face, one muscle at a time, until she could form a semblance of a smile. "That's so sweet of you to be concerned over my career, but you needn't worry yourself on my account. When I have a story to report, I always have more than enough evidence to back it up. Which reminds me, how are you expecting next month's vote on the city's zoning for low-income housing to turn out? It should be a certainty, but I understand that some of those developers have some pretty big pockets and aren't above—"

"Oh, stop it, you two," Janie said and laughed. "We're not talking business this week, and I'm not above playing the bride card if I have to and putting you both in time-out."

Janie's affection for a sister she'd never known had come easily for her, made evident when they'd met for the first time during last Saturday's custom fitting of Anna's bridesmaid's dress followed by lunch. Janie had made it clear that she already loved Anna and the two of them were going to be best friends.

This exuberance and Mary Poppins optimism had been overwhelming to Anna, who had arrived at the appointment determined to hate the spoiled sister who had grown up with all the things Anna had once coveted. Although Anna was far from calling the woman a friend, she had realized that trying to hate the younger woman would be a losing battle, and she'd have to settle for dignified indifference.

"Wait," Janie said as if finally processing Anna's and Nick's argument. "You two know each other?"

"We went to high school together," Nick said.

"Actually," Dax chimed in, "Anna and I went to high school together, too. I was a lowly freshman when you graduated, though, so I doubt you would remember, Anna."

"I'm afraid you're right," she said, even if, in fact, she did remember him, but only because when she heard that another St. Claire had started at Parrish, she'd wanted to be sure to keep her distance from him—and Kathryn St. Claire. But Dax had been harmless enough.

"And a decade later she's about to become your sister-in-law," Janie added.

God. That was true, which would mean that, technically, Nick was going to be her...brother-in-law. She worked at not visibly grimacing, which, from the look Nick was giving her, he was well aware of.

"I'm going to go out on a limb here and guess that you two didn't date," Dax teased.

"We most definitely didn't date," Nick said dryly. "Ms. Blake, here, was supposed to have been covering the student body election for the school paper when she decided to do a smear campaign on me instead."

"It was not a smear campaign. I was just doing my job," she said defensively. Wine. She needed wine. She paused and turned around, spotting the glass she'd ordered from the bartender waiting on the counter. She took a sip, giving herself a chance to calm. "I might add, however, that my source swore to me everything was true."

Everything being that Nick had been cheating off the guy's exams for more than a year and that the future student body president had paid him to write his last English Lit paper.

"Yes, perhaps he did, but had you done your due diligence, you would have seen that your source was the brother of a girl I'd dated the year before. Your reckless carelessness nearly cost me the election."

Yes, in hindsight, she had learned the importance of verifying her sources, something she never forgot again. Especially since failing to do so made her more of a social pariah than she'd already been in her worn no-name shoes and an address far from the posher zip codes where everyone else lived.

"Come on," Anna said. "Everyone knew you had that

election in the bag. Those things are more popularity contests than any kind of real testament on the merits or qualifications of the nominees. Kind of like how you got your fancy new position as the city's youngest supervisor on the board with barely any qualifications other than your last name. Must be nice to rely on your family's laurels to get what you want," she added.

The St. Claire name was as well-known and well-respected in California and on the West Coast as the Kennedy name was to Massachusetts and the East. Nick's dad had been a US senator for sixteen years, and his grandfather had been a one-term governor before that.

Her arrow seemed to have hit its mark when Nick's dark brown eyes flashed back in anger.

"Okay, okay," Dax said, not hiding his amusement at their verbal sparring. "You two definitely didn't date, and as much as I'd like to hear more, now might not be the time."

"Exactly," Janie said, ready to take the reins in the conversation. "Anna, I don't know if you had a chance to review the week's itinerary when you dropped your stuff off in your room earlier, but you might have noticed a few changes since my last email."

"Um, I'm not sure," Anna said vaguely.

She had seen a small gift basket filled with wine, chocolate, a tee shirt, and a few other odds and ends along with a detailed itinerary—a list she had purposely pushed aside. Since the moment she'd conceded to being Janie's bridesmaid, she'd been deluged with emails from the bride with questions or orders dictating how she wanted them to wear their hair, clothes to pack for the various activities that were planned for the week, what her favorite foods and colors were, and so many more that Anna had finally stopped opening them altogether. Ignorance had been bliss for as short-lived as it might have been.

"Don't worry, you can just read it later," Janie said. "The short version is that we're starting with a dance lesson in the morning, followed by lunch and a game day at the park, and then the wedding shower. Thursday morning our shuttle bus will take us on a tour of the wineries and, if we haven't had enough to drink, we'll be heading into town for the bachelor and bachelorette parties. Let me think... Oh, hot-air balloon rides on Friday morning will be capped off with a girls' day at the spa while the guys take in an afternoon of golf before the rehearsal dinner. It's a lot, I know. That's why you'll want to read that itinerary, since you wouldn't want to miss any of the fun."

Dang. Anna really should have looked at that itinerary. Dance lessons? Game day? Not to mention being stuck on a bus with all Janie's friends an entire day with no escape? Of course, Anna didn't know Janie's friends or know what they were like, but she'd met enough privileged, pretty, and popular girls in her life to know that it was unlikely they would have anything in common.

"I can hardly wait." Nick's tone didn't sound any more excited.

"There's actually one more thing," Janie said and grasped Anna's hand. "Just a tiny little thing and I wouldn't be asking this of you if it weren't an emergency." Anna didn't like the eager gleam in the younger woman's blue-gray eyes, eyes that, Anna had to admit, looked a lot like hers. "My best friend, Chantelle, was supposed to be my maid of honor, but, like a dummy, she went to Cabo this past weekend and broke her leg wakeboarding. Now she's in traction and won't be able to do any of the events that I had planned for this week."

"That's awful," Anna said, trying to appear sympathetic.

"I know. It couldn't have been timed any worse. When she called me yesterday, I thought for a moment that that was it. The start of the domino effect of what was going to be a wedding disaster. Then I had to remind myself of all the things that were right—not least of all this guy here...and you. Entering my life at this time was, like, fate. I mean, when I asked Chantelle to be my MOH last year, I didn't even know I had a sister. When you think about it, who would be more perfect for the role than you? I mean, I told myself that if you didn't show up today, I'd ask my other best friend, Sara, to stand in, but if you did, then it was meant to be. And here you are! So you'll do it? You'll be my maid of honor?"

"Maid of honor? Are you kidding—" Anna started before hearing the horror in her own tone and changed tack. "That's so sweet, but I couldn't possibly fill such big shoes. I'm sure Sara would be the better bet. She knows all about you, your friends and family, all the ins and outs of what's taking place. I mean, I don't even know the week's schedule, something that your maid of honor would need to know if she's going to help you with the planning."

"Don't be silly," Janie said. "That's what I have a wedding planner for. Lynette has already done all the legwork. All you have to do is show up with that pretty smile and hold my hand when I need it. Just like I've always wanted in a sister."

It was one thing to be part of the bridal party, one of three other bridesmaids who smiled and melded into the background. Another thing to stand up there, next to the bride in such a symbolic role. That was too much. Too much considering Anna's entire goal here had nothing to do with getting closer to Janie—except to get some dirt on her and her friends.

"Why don't we give Anna a little time to adjust to the request," Dax said, rubbing Janie's shoulder as if in a warning to dial it back. "There's no rush. Anna doesn't need to agree to anything tonight."

The guy was quickly becoming Anna's new favorite person.

His words seemed to do the trick and Janie nodded, leaning into him for a quick kiss before taking Anna's hand again and tucking it under hers. "I can't wait to introduce you to the girls. You're going to love them."

Without waiting for Anna's agreement, she pulled her along, heading directly for the bevy of bridesmaids that Anna had been trying to avoid all evening.

Well, time to put her game face on and do what she'd come here to do.

NICK COULDN'T BELIEVE his misfortune. If Anna's face as her sister dragged her away was any indication, he wasn't alone, which made him feel only slightly better.

"Crazy what a small world it is," Dax said as they watched Janie introduce Anna to the other bridesmaids.

"I'm afraid so." He really needed a drink and signaled to the bartender.

Regardless of how she tried to deflect any blame now, Anna Blake had nearly cost him his first election, which, at the time, had felt like the most important thing in his life. His anger, frustration, and yes, even fear—fear of losing and disappointing his parents—had been real. That same fear never really left him.

It was why Anna's sudden presence here again at such a pivotal time in his political career—when he was just days away from announcing his candidacy in the soon-to-be-vacant California Senate seat thanks to the retirement of Senator Hartley—could spell disaster. Nick had thought he was going to have to wait another four years before attempting to make the jump from San Francisco's city supervisor to a larger election like the state senate.

As ready as Nick was to make his candidacy announcement, he also knew that, out of courtesy for his brother and Janie, he needed to keep the news on the down low. He wouldn't want to risk overshadowing the wedding. This week was about Dax's wedding and nothing else.

And was precisely why he needed to stay clear of Anna Blake.

Nick was well aware of the type of news that places like *The Daily Rundown* put out. Dirt and gossip that she dressed up as "entertainment news" but at its heart was nothing more than tabloid trash.

Taking his drink, he and Dax discussed stats from last week's Giants game as he tried to distract himself from the growing group of bridesmaids several yards away. Four in total—including Anna—to match Dax's four groomsmen. With a wary eye, he watched Sara cast a glance his way before disengaging from the group and heading in his direction. There was no avoiding her now. It was probably for the best. Get it over and done with.

She was wearing her dark brown hair shorter now, so that the waves fell just above her shoulders, giving her the appearance of sweetness that one might believe was sincere —if they didn't look too far underneath the surface. It wasn't like Sara had suddenly taken off her mask when they were dating, showing him exactly why they were wrong for each other. No, she'd been more subtle than that. Sara had perfected the art of making sly insults buried beneath compliments and not to mention passive-aggressive behavior that she used to get what she wanted.

Then there was the additional fact that just weeks after they started dating, rumors about their supposed fairy-tale romance were everywhere. By the time he finally called it off, there were even rumors of a ring and an imminent wedding somewhere in Ireland. None of which was remotely true, and it wasn't hard to figure out where the leaks had originated.

"Nicholas St. Claire, are you going to hide from me all night?"

"Not at all. How are you, Sara?" he asked politely.

"I'm doing all right. Much better now, though." Without asking, she grabbed his drink, letting the glass linger against her lips before taking a generous sip and handing it back.

Nick glanced at Dax, who shrugged and seemed anxious to get away. "I should probably go see if the rest of the guys are almost here," he said before patting Nick on the shoulder and walking away.

Traitor. Nick never would have gotten tangled up with Sara DeWinters in the first place if he hadn't agreed to join Dax and Janie for drinks that unfortunate night.

"What do think about this long-lost sister of Janie's?" she asked, turning her attention to the woman whose hand was still grasped in Janie's, offering her no chance at escape. "I hear she's a reporter for one of those gossip rags."

"I'm still trying to figure her out. See if she's here for the right reasons."

"Good idea. Did you hear she's actually asked her to take Chantelle's role as maid of honor? Not that I care, even if I have known her since we were in third grade and was there when she and Dax first met."

"I don't think you have anything to worry about on that score. She didn't sound like she was interested in the position."

"Or so she pretended. You know that there are rumors that a reporter from the *LA Times* might actually be covering the wedding. I would bet she's angling for the spot so she can milk the publicity a little longer, maybe get a trade up from where she currently works."

"I guess we'll see," he said noncommittally, even if he had to admit that Sara might be on to something. From his vantage point, Anna didn't look particularly eager to be here, let alone be part of the bridal party for a woman she hadn't met until last week. Curious.

Nick was saved from further conversation by the roar of the arriving groomsman who ran out onto the courtyard and tackled the groom to the ground in a loud and macho display of masculine energy.

"Have a good one, Sara," Nick said, and before she could say anything more to keep his attention, he headed over to greet the new guests, even as Sara's words about the bride's sister stuck in his mind.

One thing was certain. Nick would definitely be keeping an eye on the woman, making sure she didn't start any trouble.

ANNA TRIED to remember the last name of the bridesmaid she'd met earlier that night. Megan. Megan...Hellerman. That was it.

She typed it into the Google search bar and waited. After

a few minutes of reading about the one bridesmaid who'd actually smiled with sincerity when she was introduced, Anna pushed the computer away in disgust and sank back onto the plush queen bed.

This assignment was going to be harder than she'd thought. It was one thing to dish the dirt and details when she was merely an observer, her motives always clear that she was getting the dirt for the specific purpose of publishing. It was another thing entirely to subtly fish for the information in the guise of someone who might be a friend.

A roar of laugher from outside her open window told her that the first party of the week was still going strong, even if the sun had slipped behind the hills hours ago.

Mildly curious, Anna slipped off the bed and went over to the window to look out. The pool was glowing beyond the courtyard, and she could make out people milling on the lawn and in the pool, not to mention a tennis court located farther behind she hadn't noticed before.

What would it have been like to live in this place? Have servants available to answer her every wish? Money to buy anything she desired? A mother *and a father* ready to shower her with love and devotion?

There was a loud splash as someone was thrown into the pool. After having spent the past few hours meeting every member of the wedding party and making the usual small talk about where everyone was from, how they knew the bride and groom, what if anything they did for a living, Anna finally had to withdraw from the party to recharge her battery. She was physically and emotionally drained. And it was only the first night.

At least she'd been spared having to meet any relatives other than Janie. Most of them wouldn't be arriving until Friday, giving her time to acclimate a little better to her surroundings...and to her sister. As to the bride's mother's whereabouts, according to Megan, she was off at some plush Parisian retreat getting something or other rejuvenated.

For a minute, she considered calling Tessa and Quinn, her two best friends and roommates, just to hear their supportive voices, but quickly dismissed the idea. Quinn was prepping for a big trial, and if she had any spare time, she was probably enjoying it with her new and utterly devoted boyfriend. Tessa, who Anna had hitched a ride with out of the city, undoubtedly had her hands full with whatever crisis her brothers had that called her home to the family farm in Sonoma.

Instead, Anna lingered by the window a little longer, seeing if she could identify any of the guests below. She spotted Megan, Trish, and Sara, her fellow bridesmaids, standing alongside the pool, watching as two of the groomsmen wrestled in the water. She was still trying to straighten out the groomsmen and their names, but they all seemed laid-back, and she knew it would be easy hanging out with them.

Janie and Dax were seated in one of the chaises, his arms around her as they laughed and whispered together, lost in their own world. For a moment, she remembered Janie's crestfallen face when, around ten, Anna announced she was heading to bed. The woman had clearly hoped they might have had more time to chat, something that Anna had assured her they'd have plenty of time to do before she headed up to her room to decompress.

Nick was sitting in a chair a few feet away from the love-birds, his attention immersed in whatever was on the phone screen lit up before him rather than the horseplay around him. Single-minded and focused. That's what she remembered about him from high school, too. In his studies, his spot on the school's swim team that took them to state, and on anything he set his mind to having. Like that election.

Not that he didn't have moments where he got... distracted. Key point, the fact the guy had dated probably half of the entire female population of Parrish Hall at one time or another. The beautiful and popular half, that was. A population that Anna definitely had not belonged in.

No, she was more the studious type, a loner with few friends and no interests outside of her job on the school paper. A girl who Nick and his friends had laughed at for being a little too weird, too intense, and too outspoken to be accepted into the in crowd.

She'd come a long way since high school, fortunately. But not long enough not to remember the sting of feeling like she didn't belong.

Anna glanced back at her computer still out on the bed, knowing that she couldn't let those feelings of inadequacy resurface, not when she needed to appear to be like everyone else—that was, if she hoped to find anything worthwhile to bring to Charlie.

And the only way she could do that was if she kept her distance from Nick St. Claire, a guy who only reminded her of her former inadequacies and insecurities.

A guy who still could make her feel like she wasn't good enough.

CHAPTER 3

INSANITY. That was what this was. Who scheduled group dance lessons at eight thirty in the morning?

Anna stifled a yawn as she made her way down the stairs and into the now empty dining room, where she found the remnants of the eight o'clock breakfast she'd missed when she'd pushed snooze one too many times on her alarm. A morning person she was not.

Anna looked over what was left of the spread. Muffins, fruit, waffles, and two domed lids that, when she looked underneath, revealed rubbery-looking scrambled eggs and sausage. She stabbed a piece of melon and stuffed it into her mouth before grabbing a hand full of cheese cubes and looking around for signs of coffee.

Nice. A Keurig. At least she could guarantee her coffee was fresh and hot.

"Late riser, are we?"

She didn't have to turn around to know whose voice that was, and she shrugged, not seeing why she had to offer any excuses to him.

Before Nick could comment again, she pushed the brew button, glad for the machine's whirling that drowned out the possibility for any conversation. She stuffed two cheese cubes in her mouth while it finished brewing, hoping to avoid further discussion.

"Maybe tomorrow you could deign to join the rest of us for breakfast. I know Janie would certainly appreciate it."

Seriously? She'd slept through her alarm, not that she should have to give him any excuses. "Why, Nick, I didn't realize that my whereabouts were of such interest to you. Did you miss me? Is that it?" she asked, looking up to flutter her eyes at him.

Merciful Lord.

It was a kick to the gut to see him here, in the flesh again, after all these years. The years had been too kind to the guy. Figured.

She did a sweeping inventory of his many attributes.

Dark brown hair, thick and wavy. A hard, stubborn jawline that, even now, flexed as if he was gritting his teeth. Full, sensuous lips that had no business existing on such a brooding face. But it was his eyes that were the most memorable of all. Dark molten brown that glared unforgivingly at her. Although, today, there was something else in those depths other than anger and annoyance that she couldn't figure out.

She turned away to grab her coffee, needing a reprieve from the intensity of his gaze.

"Ordinarily, I couldn't care less about your whereabouts, Ms. Blake. My only concern is that my brother, Dax, and his fiancée have a fun, relaxing week celebrating with their friends and family in the days leading up to their wedding. And for now, that concern involves you in as much as Janie wants you present and participating to make this week perfect. Now that we've identified my concern, maybe we can discuss yours. What exactly are your motives in coming here? What angle are you playing?"

"What do you mean?" she asked as innocently as possible. "Janie's my sister and you said it yourself, she wants me here as much as I want to be here." Okay, so everything up to that last part had been true. "My, you've become paranoid in your old age, St. Claire. Just because I didn't collapse in a fit of tears when Janie and I were reunited doesn't mean I'm not happy to be part of her special day."

"Paranoid or not, I have reason to be when it comes to anything that involves you," he said in a dangerously raspy tone.

"You flatter me. I didn't know I wielded such power over you."

"I'd hardly consider—"

Whatever witty words Nick was going to say next were lost when a hulking mass of testosterone wrapped his arms tightly around Nick's before pulling him down to the floor. The shock on Nick's usually composed face as he went down almost made the entirety of this week worth it, and she didn't try to hide her laughter at his momentary bewilderment.

It took Nick about three seconds to regain his faculties and flip the guy over, pinning his arm behind him.

"You're losing your touch, dude," the guy said from the ground before Nick released him and they came to their feet, both grinning. "Once upon a time, you'd have had me *before* you hit the ground."

"I was distracted," Nick said.

The new guy turned to look at her for the first time, his

smile broadening as he did. "I'd say. And who exactly is this beautiful...distraction?"

For almost twenty years of Anna's life, she'd never been even remotely considered beautiful and to hear the words now could still be something of a shock. Not that she had been a real eyesore or anything as a kid, but she had suffered a long stretch of awkward years, with the usual stringy, flat hair, bad teeth and acne, and the thin, scrawny figure of a prepubescent girl for longer than she'd have liked.

It took somewhere around her twenty-first birthday for the curves to come in, both top and bottom, and for her to find the calming influence of running to help keep her sane, healthy, and far more confident.

The confidence came easier now, and she was used to the compliments and attention, even used it to her benefit when necessary. Especially when trying to convince a source to share more than he should. However, under the watchful glare of the guy who'd known her back before the transformation, hearing a compliment felt different. Almost embarrassing.

Anna looked over the beefy guy who'd managed to take Nick down a peg or two with interest. The guy was hot in that overblown muscle-man kind of way with light brown hair, hazel eyes, and an easy grin. He was the exact type of guy she usually went for. Not necessarily the brightest, but always fun and—more importantly—uncomplicated.

She smiled, ready to find her own traction again. "Anna Blake. And you are?"

"Chris Walker. Groomsman extraordinaire. A little late to the party but something I'm glad to have rectified."

Chris Walker. The name was familiar. "As in linebacker for the New England Patriots Chris Walker?"

"So you've heard of me," he said, grinning wickedly. Oh, he was a charmer.

"Who hasn't?" Nick said, sounding impatient. "Now that the introductions are over, we should probably join everyone else."

"Don't worry about St. Claire, Anna. As uptight as he is, he sometimes forgets how to behave in front of a beautiful woman."

"I definitely won't worry about St. Claire," she said, amping up her smile to a megawatt volume. "I'm well aware of how uptight he can be."

She could feel Nick's ire from two feet away.

Chris chuckled. "Well, before we get too sidetracked, the future bride actually sent me here to retrieve you both. Would you be so kind as to let me escort you?" he asked, offering her his arm.

Without another glance at Nick, he led the way down the hall and toward the sunroom, where the clamor of voices and laughter was hard to miss. The bright room that had been filled with chairs and rugs last night was now cleared of everything except for the groomsmen and brides-maids, who were chattering happily amongst themselves.

"Anna! There you are," Janie cried and waved her over.

With a grateful smile and wave to Chris, she headed over to her sister, determined not to flinch when the smaller woman hugged her exuberantly again, especially when she was certain that Nick St. Claire was watching her more care-fully than he should. "I want you to meet Lynette. She's my wedding planner and dance teacher extraordinaire, who I'd be totally lost without. Lynette, this is my sister, Anna."

Anna turned to the woman, a petite redhead with a quick smile and a tight handshake that left Anna's arm socket a little sore. "Nice to meet you, Anna." Not waiting a beat, she clapped her hands together to get the room's attention. "Good morning, everyone! It's nice to see such enthusiasm for today's lesson. Now, we have a lot to learn this morning if you're going to get the steps down by Saturday, so lets get started."

"What exactly are we learning?" one of the groomsmen called out. Josh, was it?

"Are we doing some kind of flash mob dance?" Megan asked.

"Not exactly. At the reception, Janie and Dax will open the dancing with the couple's first dance, a fun swing number that we've been working on for weeks. You all will be joining them about three minutes in. Don't worry, I'll show you exactly what we have in mind. You're all going to look great."

Anna's belly sank. Swing dancing? That sounded far more complicated than she, the woman with two left feet, was capable of.

"What I need is for the women to line up first, and I'll show you the basic steps. Then we'll have the guys line up for the same. Once we have the steps down, you'll join your partner so we can move on to a few more advanced moves. It's going to be a piece of cake, I promise." She clapped her hands again and moved to the center of the floor. "Ladies, line up here, please. Janie, you join them, too."

Good grief. Let the humiliation begin.

Anna watched as Lynette moved deftly back and forth and then sashayed to the left, vocalizing her steps as she did so. She did it two more times, and Anna was aware of the other women already starting to move with her, their bodies rocking with the beat.

Seriously? Was she the only woman lacking the dancing chromosome?

"Remember, ladies," Lynette called out, "we will always start with the right foot. Okay, now let's all try it together. Keeping your weight on your left foot, take a step back with your right foot. Now, step that right foot forward. It's a rock step. Let's do it a few more times. Back and forward."

Okay. This seemed easy enough. Back and forth. Back and forth.

"Excellent! Now we're going to move on. When you step forward, don't plant your foot, because we're going to take three steps to your right. So, rock back, step forward, and then side, together, side. And back, and then rock step again."

Wait. What?

She tried to imitate the woman but fell to the right not so gracefully. Again. The next time she put an extra step in. Crap.

"Anna. Anna. Look at me," Lynette said in a patient tone. "Rock, step, side, close, side. Rock, step, side, close, side."

She was well aware of how clumsy she was and how every other woman there already had the basic move down. From the corner of her eye, she caught Nick watching her with a dangerous shine in his eyes. Had he smiled, she might have gone over and kicked him.

Anna lost her focus and stepped with the wrong foot, landing on Sara's foot next to her. "Oh! Sorry!"

"I think we're getting it, ladies," Lynette said, not meeting Anna's gaze. "Let's move to the side and keep practicing, but for now, guys? Let's line you up."

Now this should be good. Men were renowned for not easily keeping the beat. She had to be better than them, right? Particularly Nick St. Claire.

Lynette explained the steps, which were essentially the mirror image of the ladies', starting with stepping the left foot back. Anna smiled while anticipating the train wreck about to happen, her focus most particularly on Nick, who...

Nailed it.

Of course he did. To rub the salt in deeper, he turned and gave her a gloating smile as if he knew she'd been waiting for him to fail.

"I think we've got the idea. Okay. It's time to partner up," Lynette instructed.

Partner up? Anna glanced over the group, wondering who she'd torment with her painfully awkward dance movements. Jake and Josh she'd met last night, but she was pretty certain that Megan already had her eye on Jake, and Josh—

A thick pair of hands grabbed her by the waist and she squealed.

"No worries, Anna," Chris said and winked at her. "You're with me."

Anna turned to see how the rest of the group partnered up, noticing immediately how Janie's maid-of-honor runner up, Sara, headed directly toward Nick.

Having done more digging last night into the bridal party's history, Anna wasn't surprised. If the gossip was to be believed, he and Sara had been quite the item last year, even on the verge of their own engagement when it all fell apart for unknown reasons and they went their separate ways. Nick's jaw was set in that familiar grimace as Sara planted herself in front of him.

"All right. Now let's give it a whirl. And..." Lynette counted off the steps again, this time watching and walking around the room to coach everyone along.

Oof. Chris's foot landed on hers.

"Sorry." He grinned, looking abashed. Seconds later, it was her turn to apologize when she landed on his foot.

Meeting each other's eyes, they burst into laughter. They tried the steps again, this time each moving with the wrong foot before laughter overcame them.

"Wonderful, you two, you're dancing beautifully," Lynette said. But she was talking about Nick and Sara, who were moving together in total sync. Show-offs.

Her attention broken, she stepped on Chris's foot, who didn't seem to mind as he continued counting his own steps under his breath. Maybe this wasn't going to be so bad after all. At least she had a partner in crime in her ineptitude.

"Hold up, everyone." Lynette was looking at Anna and Chris with a speculative gleam. "I think we need to do a little shake-up. Anna? Sara? Could you two ladies switch partners for me?"

No. No no no no no.

From the look on Sara's face, she didn't appear any happier about the order.

"Come on. Quickly, ladies. I want to try an experiment."

Not seeing much choice, Anna walked across the room to stand next to Nick, whose face turned into a mask as she drew near.

"We know that Nick and Sara have the moves down beautifully, so let's see if we can take Anna's and Chris's dancing up a little higher. Now, let's try it again."

She had to touch Nick. No, not just touch him, but rest her right hand over his while her left arm rested on his other arm.

"Let's just get this over with," he muttered and held his hand out.

Anna took his hand, highly aware of his other hand resting on her left shoulder blade, something that hadn't bothered her with Chris but, with this man, felt entirely too intimate. She tried to relax, sure he could feel her tension as they moved to the steps as Lynette called them out. If Nick noticed her distress, he didn't give any indication.

If he could be so unaffected by this intimacy, so could she. She smiled.

Immediately Nick lost his footing.

"Is there a problem?" she asked.

His hand tightened over hers. "Just that whenever you smile, I immediately grow nervous."

Noted. She'd definitely have to smile more often around him.

Lynette recounted the steps, and when Anna stepped back, she was surprised to see Nick move back in perfect time with her. When she moved forward, he was there, just as when he guided her to her right with the side steps.

"Much better! Wonderful" Lynette cried. "Pay attention, everyone. The person you're dancing with right now is going to be your partner for the big dance. I know things are going to be busy over the next few days until the reception on Saturday, but I expect all of you to find the time to work together and finesse your moves. Okay. Let's try it again, everyone, only this time I'm going to add music. Then we can experiment with some turns."

Permanent? She was stuck with him?

Smile, Anna. Don't let him know you've just entered the seventh circle of hell.

NICK WAS ANNOYED. Annoyed as much at Anna as he was himself. Letting her get to him like she was. After everything she'd done to him, almost destroying not just his chance at the student body president but his reputation and entire high school career, Nick should be barely tolerating holding this woman so closely to him.

Not be wondering things like why she smelled as sweet and fresh as she did or whether she would flash those pretty eyes at him in anger if he pointed out how she'd missed the beat three of the last five counts.

He needed to hear her say something ridiculous so he could go back to his safe feelings of justified anger.

"Tell me about yourself, Anna. How did a girl who once aimed for working for *The New York Times* find herself writing frivolous gossip bites for *The Daily Rundown*?"

That did the trick, as Anna's eyes narrowed and she glared at him. Only, in the process, her anger also flushed her cheeks, making those same eyes shimmer. "I wasn't aware that you followed my work so closely."

He hadn't, at least not until he returned to his room last night and looked her up. He had to admit, despite the shallowness of the topics, her stories were all well written and had that easy-to-read flow that would suck people in. She always had been a good storyteller.

"I had some time on my hands," he said vaguely. "Don't tell me, you were fired from a job working for a larger paper because you forgot to verify your sources? Maybe got the paper sued for libel?"

"Funny," she said.

Nick reached for her other hand and they practiced another turn. He noticed that, now distracted from her nervousness, she was actually improving.

"Not that it's your business," Anna continued, "but you'd be surprised at the number of new journalists who graduate with a degree every year, all vying for a few ever-dwindling job opportunities. But I haven't given up. Who knows, I might be the staff writer on the *LA Times* who gets the chance to write about your fall from grace in another ten years."

He bit back a smile. "Not a chance. So tell me more about how this entertainment news beat of yours works? Because for someone who pretends not to know a lot about me or what I've been up to over the years, the St. Claire name has certainly popped up on more than a few occasions in your circulation."

"We have more than one person on staff," she said sharply. "Fortunately, the news as it's related to the more... local celebrities and personalities, usually gets covered by some of the less-experienced staff."

"Ah. So you're so good at dredging up the muck that you get to dredge the muck on the big hitters. How...impressive."

"I guess if I had a parent who had the right connections, a name that resounded with readers, you know, something like how you started your own career off right out of the gate, my prospects would have been better. But everything I have, everything that I've written and where I am is because of my efforts, my work alone. And that's enough for me."

Nick couldn't argue there. He sometimes wondered whether he would have taken the win as city supervisor a couple of years ago had he not had the family name. But he wasn't going to deny his roots, deny his family's political renown to satisfy his ego. He just counted himself lucky. But Anna wasn't as nameless as she pretended. Not anymore.

"Well, now you're something of a celebrity within your own right, wouldn't you say? After the story that ran in the *Chronicle*, people know who you are. They know your father. Are you saying that if the *Times* came knocking at your door tomorrow because they'd seen your story and wanted to hire you—writing under the Van Hollins name, of course—you wouldn't jump at the chance, even though you knew that you only got it because of your father's name?"

Instead of an easy denial, a claim that she would never sink so low as to rely solely on her family's laurels to move ahead, Anna's brow crunched up as she considered this.

"Interesting dilemma, isn't it?" he asked, unable to help himself as he savored this small victory of having quite possibly got the better of the woman.

"Not a dilemma at all. I would never, not even for a minute, take possession of that name. The man didn't deign to give it to me when he was alive, and I would never take it now on his death, no matter what it might afford me. I will never be a Van Hollins," she said vehemently.

The force with which she said the words left him little doubt she meant what she'd said. The history of her father's not recognizing her, acknowledging she was his, was not water under the bridge. Enough that she would cut off her nose to spite her face if the opportunity arose.

He supposed he couldn't blame her. Nick had no qualms about his family name because he was proud of it, proud of his connection to such men and women who had done so many positive things for others.

Anna had no reason to feel similar pride or connection to the Van Hollins name or family. She'd as much as said so.

"Then that begs the question," he said softly, "if you eschew the Van Hollins name so much, and all that it represents, then...why are you here? Why would you want to help the other daughter of the man who so obviously slighted you for all these years?"

The guilt that crossed her face in that moment was all the confirmation that Nick needed. He'd been right. There was another reason she was here, and he was going to find out.

But by the set of Anna's jaw as she glared at him, he knew that he wouldn't be finding out anything more from her right now. He had time, however.

Nick smiled. The prospect of ferreting that truth out of this spirited and stubborn reporter was something he might even look forward to.

CHAPTER 4

"I CAN'T BELIEVE that with eleven seconds on the clock, you guys still ran that play," Josh was telling Chris in between bites of his second burger.

Anna was finishing up her own hamburger that Janie's catering staff had grilled up for today's picnic at a neighborhood park, pretending that she knew what they were talking about, when a text came in on her cell phone.

It was an alert from a source she'd used a few times in the past saying he had something hot if Anna was interested. With Chris sitting far too close to her to be able to text anything in private, Anna excused herself from the table and walked a few feet away to call the guy instead.

"Jeff? It's Anna. What do you have for me?"

There was a shuffle on the other end and she guessed that Jeff was finding somewhere to talk to her in private. Jeff was an aide to one of the local state senators and was one of her best assets with his rare but juicy gossip, all of which, so far, had turned out to be one hundred percent accurate. Like the state congressman who had an illicit affair with his campaign manager despite his wife recently giving birth to twins. Or the wife of a conservative anti-immigrant televangelist, who had donated thousands of dollars to several state senators and had been caught stepping out with their strapping young Honduran landscaper.

Anna needed a win, and she held her breath with the hope this could be the break she needed.

"I just caught wind that Senator Hartley is suffering from some personal health issues and there's talk that he's going to be announcing his retirement next week."

Senator Hartley retiring? That was news since the guy was a polarizing figure in local politics. His announcement would galvanize half of his constituents with relief and the other half with bitter disappointment. Hmm. She was going to need to confirm this with someone else, maybe—

"There's something else." He waited, and his voice dropped. "There's been some mention that the party has already approached a prominent local figure to run, and that this person has agreed, but he's asked that nothing go public until after this week."

"Who is it? Do you know?"

"Not yet. I'll keep working on it. But the party thinks the guy is on his way up, some political legacy."

Legacy? "Okay. Thanks, Jeff. I owe you big."

Anna hung up the phone but didn't return to the group as she considered what Jeff had said. Big name. A local guy. Couldn't announce anything until after this—

No way. It couldn't be.

But her gut instinct was telling her not to dismiss the possibility. She glanced over to where he was sitting.

Sure enough, Nick St. Claire was watching her with undisguised curiosity. He'd been doing that since the minute she got here. She'd thought he was paranoid, that it was a reflection of how things had last gone down between them. But maybe it was something more. Maybe Nick had a secret and that was why he was so determined to watch her closely.

Okay, that was a lot of ifs and guesses and hunches. The only way she was really going to know was if she asked him. Or at least hinted at it, giving her a chance to gauge his reaction.

Pocketing the phone, she returned to the group, where everyone was digging into a pile of decadent-looking brownies. Instead of taking her seat next to Chris, however, she continued on past Jake and Megan, who seemed to be hitting it off, and over to the other side of the table. She stood next to him, waiting for him to notice her standing there, which he did after another few seconds. Begrudgingly, he moved a few inches over so she could sit on the corner of the bench.

"How was your lunch?" she asked, deciding now was as good a time as any to start gauging his responses for honesty.

"Delicious. How was your call?"

"Illuminating."

"Yeah, well, maybe you should be paying more attention to the bride and the events going on around you, not taking phone calls that couldn't possibly have anything to do with what we're doing here. I mean, as you said, you are here for Janie. Because she means so much to you, right?"

His tone suggested he thought she was full of it. She could play the same game, however. "Right. I mean, now that Janie and I have found each other, it goes without saying that we're going to be spending a lot of time together in the future. Her new family and the events going on in their lives are going to affect her and, by extension, me. Wouldn't you agree?"

That was pretty ingenious. The way she turned it around on him like that, and she congratulated herself on getting closer to where she needed to go with this questioning, hoping to move on to what new events he, as Janie's brother-in-law, might be getting involved in.

"No, I don't agree," he said bluntly. "Since we both know that once you get whatever you're angling for here, you're going to be pulling up those roots you pretend to be nurturing and heading back to your life, with barely a thought to Janie or anyone else. So, no. Nothing that Janie's new family may or may not do is likely to make any difference in your life."

Darn. Why did he have to be so suspicious? Anna glanced around the table, worried that someone might have overheard the jerk and might now be looking at her just as suspiciously. But everyone was caught up in their conversations and gave them no mind. Well, everyone but Sara, but she was too far away to have heard anything.

"Look, Nick. I don't know what you want from me. I'm here, I'm trying to do the right thing by Janie, making sure she gets the dream wedding, the dream sister, the dream everything that she's ever wanted. I think you can cut me a little slack."

"Really? You think you're doing everything you can here? Because I think you've been doing the bare minimum to get by. You don't think I—or Janie—noticed the way you escaped the party early last night or how you skipped out on breakfast? Or how, whenever Janie hugs you, you look like you're willing yourself not to flee? You're passing time here on your way to something else and we both know it. A story, perhaps? Is that it? You're supposed to be using your connections to get the dirt on Janie and her friends?"

Holy crap. Had she been that obvious? Nick had just laid

it all out there, seeing through her like plastic wrap. But she was nothing if not a good denier.

"You're wrong. Completely wrong. I left early last night because I was exhausted, having spent hours surrounded by people I don't know, all of whom were likely judging me, wondering why Malcolm never embraced me or even acknowledged me as his daughter during his life, and I needed some quiet time to myself." Time to wonder the very same questions, not to mention wonder who she was going to stab in the back for her story. "And this morning I freaking slept through the alarm—hardly intentional. But I'm here and smiling and trying to make the best of the situation, trying to act like I belong, so I would love it if you would lay off me for two seconds."

Anna didn't know where that had come from, but she knew that although she'd started her explanation as a way to weasel out of his accusation, somewhere in the answer, she found herself stating something closer to the truth.

People were judging her, wondering why she was here. Wondering what was wrong with her, and it was exhausting, not helped by the fact she was being duplicitous, trying to work her way into their graces for a bit of truth that she was going to use against them.

At this rate, she wasn't going to make it to the end of the week. She didn't know if she'd make it through the freaking day. A suspicious heat hit her eyes, and she blinked quickly, hoping that Nick didn't see what had been the start of tears.

Getting up, Anna grabbed her phone out of her pocket again and walked a few feet away, keeping her back to the group. She needed a moment to pull herself together, and if she was lucky, should anyone be watching her, they might think she was simply responding to a text.

What the heck was coming over her? She didn't cry. She was tougher than that.

It was all Nick's fault. He was the one pushing her, making her feel crummier with his pointed questions. Making her even feel...guilty.

THE TEARS that rose to Anna's eyes had been unmistakable. Combined with the truth of what she'd said, of people, not just him, suspicious of her motives for being here, made Nick feel about one inch tall.

He got up from the table and followed her to where she was standing. "Hey. I'm sorry."

She didn't look up. "You should be."

"Don't get me wrong. I still think you're up to something, that's true. But I failed to take into account that being here might be costing you something personally, too." He paused, struggling. "Look. We can't keep butting heads like we're doing, not if we're going to survive this week without bringing everyone into our drama. We need to reach some sort of compromise if this is going to work."

"Compromise? Like what?" she asked, raising her gaze to his.

Yeah, they'd been tears. But even the pink tinge around her eyes couldn't take away from their lovely blue depths.

Time to be up-front. "I guess the best way to figure that out is if we each lay our cards on the table as to what we want, what each of us needs this week for us to see it as a success. Only then can we negotiate."

"Good idea. So what do you want, Nick? What is it that I could possibly do here that would put an end to your suspicions?"

That one was easy. "I want this week to be the most memorable and happiest week of my brother's and his fiancée's lives, without any snafus, without having to worry that anyone might be trying to undermine them or their happiness by, say, selling them or their friends out."

"Really? That's all you want," she said in a tone that suggested she didn't believe him. "That call I took earlier? It was from one of my most reliable sources. Someone who seems to think that the sleeper election season that everyone is expecting might become more spirited after a certain long-term state senator gives his retirement announcement next week."

He put on his poker face. "Really? Anyone I know?"

"I believe so." She tilted her head as she studied him. "But that's not the kicker. There are rumors that the party has already found their candidate to run for the seat and that they're ready to throw all their support behind this guy. Some legacy as I hear it. Are you sure you don't know anything about this?"

Damn. Where did she get this stuff? Nick glanced at her phone, almost wanting to sneak it away just to see the name of this so-called source.

But that was beside the point. The point was Anna was on to him and if she kept digging, she'd find the confirmation she needed to blow the lid off of this story, and there would go his hope of letting Dax and Janie enjoy this week in solitude.

"Funny, but I don't remember breaking political news was something that usually reached the gossip column of *The Daily Rundown*. That's kind of far afield of your specialty, wouldn't you say?"

"News is news. And if this is true, and I bring it to my editor to break before anyone else, then my job will be secure, and I won't need to dredge up any old secrets from the other attendees here."

"So I was right. You are here because you need a story." He hit on something else she said. "Why would your job be on the line, though?"

She paused, as if debating what she wanted to share with him. "Let's just say that my editor didn't take it very well when our competitor broke the news about Malcolm Van Hollins's illegitimate love child before we did—despite my being said illegitimate love child."

"She was going to fire you over that?" Okay, so Nick had known that Anna was up to something, and for a few seconds, he'd been elated to know he'd been right. She had wanted a story, something to further her career, as always. Only, from the sound of it, she needed something not to further her career but rather to save it.

"Of course she was. It's my job to deliver scoops on things like that, regardless of my personal interest."

Nick didn't know if he agreed with that. There had to be some limits, but it wasn't for him to say. Instead, he'd focus on working this out so they could stop being at each other's throats and get what they needed to make this week a success. "What if I told you that I'd be willing to not only go on the record to confirm this tip that you're working but that I'd give you an exclusive first interview on the topic, one that I know any other newspaper would be dying to get?"

"I'd say...I'm listening. What's the catch?"

"The catch is that you can't release this story until after the wedding and after the happy couple have slipped away with perfect memories of their big day, untarnished by reports of my campaign hovering over the week. And..." he added when she smiled too smugly, apparently under the impression that was the extent of his terms, "you are going to tell Janie how touched and honored you are that she asked you to play such an important role in her wedding and that you would love to be her maid of honor."

He let that sink in for a minute.

She wasn't smiling any longer, but she also wasn't throwing the offer back at him. Instead, she seemed to be thinking it over. "So all I have to do is agree to be the maid of honor and hold off on printing the story until after Saturday, and you'll give me the exclusive."

He shook his head, grinning. "Not quite. You won't be just accepting the title of maid of honor, but you're going to be the epitome of what a maid of honor should be: totally dedicated to the bride. In other words, if Janie asks you to sit next to her on the bus and hold her hand, then you're going to sit next to her, hold her hand, and offer to rub her back, too. If she wants you to play a rousing game of Truth or Dare, or even sing naked karaoke at some dive bar at her bachelorette party, you're going to do precisely that, even if it means you breaking into "We Are Family" in your birthday suit. Although, make sure I'm there for that last one."

He threw that in as a joke to see how fast it took for her right eye to begin twitching, something it seemed to do when she was seriously annoyed. Usually with him. But Nick had to admit, seeing her naked wouldn't be the worst thing in the world. Okay, it would be pretty damned good. It was hard to miss the fact that the skinny, hardheaded adolescent girl who had tried to sabotage his senior year had turned into a gorgeous woman with a killer smile, killer legs, and a bra cup now larger than mosquito bites.

He was a Neanderthal. He could own that. "So, do we have a deal?"

She looked thoughtful. "I'm going to need to interview you if I'm going to put together any kind of decent story."

"Of course. I'll give you ten minutes every day, provided you're keeping up your end of the bargain."

"Fifteen minutes. Starting tonight."

"All right. Fifteen." He was nothing but amenable. "We can meet after the bridal shower is over and you've shown Janie that you're here and invested in being part of this whole thing."

She nodded. "Okay. Then I guess we have a deal."

Tentatively, she reached her hand out to him and, unable to help himself, he smiled as he took it, enjoying the softness of her skin, the weight of her hand in his, just as he had when they'd danced earlier.

That wasn't good. This was about a bargain, an agreement. Nothing more.

Keep your head in the game, Nick.

"Hey, lovebirds," Dax shouted from the field where everyone had congregated since he and Anna started their discussion. "Get out here so we can this game started already."

With an agreement in place, one that he was sure would give them both what they needed, which would assure him a little peace for the next few days, Nick smiled. "Ready to have your ass handed to you?"

"I don't know. Are you?" she asked, her hand on her hip.

Let the games begin.

∼

"ONE WEDDING BELL. Two wedding bells. Three wedding bells," Janie hollered, singing the countdown she'd mandated for today's game.

Nick sized up the competition on team "pink"—or so the bedazzled tee shirts its members wore said, thanks to Janie's skills with a glue gun. Chris, Josh, Trish, and Anna glared fiercely at him and the blue team as Janie counted. Nick just hoped that Jake and Megan would stop with the flirting and focus on what was happening on the field.

He meant to win this thing.

"Break!"

That was the defense's cue to charge the other team and the lucky person who might be carrying the ball. In this case, it was Chris, which meant an all-out fight to tag the professional football player, who thought he couldn't lose. Nick sprinted after the guy who, although fast, had been too cocky and miscalculated how close Nick was to overtaking him.

Or so Nick thought until the moment Chris tossed the ball directly to Anna, who was just outside the end zone. In two seconds, she crossed the line, making the touchdown.

Damn.

Winded, Nick paused to catch his breath, unable to miss Chris charging Anna and picking her up in a roar of excitement. To Nick's surprise, instead of ordering the hulk to put her down, she laughed out loud, her head falling back as if she was actually enjoying the moment. For reasons Nick couldn't identify, the action pissed him off.

He gritted his teeth as Chris slid Anna down his side and back to the ground, the blonde smiling and pushing at his shoulder flirtatiously. How the hell had she learned to turn up the charm like that? It was almost like...like she was enjoying the attention.

Ignoring the couple, he joined his team's huddle, where, with only five minutes left, a winning strategy was the priority. "All right. Remember, get in T formation and do whatever you have to to stop Chris from getting through. Jake? Megan? Be ready."

They lined up again, Dax ready to count down and put the ball into play. It was hard to miss the shine of excitement that flashed across Anna's face as she stared directly at him.

Nick immediately had his defenses up. But the ball was in play in the next second and he didn't have time to think about it as Dax threw it to Jake, their decoy, and Nick raced to get into position. As planned, Jake handed the ball off to Megan, and just when the heat was on her, she stopped, took aim, and threw it back in Nick's direction.

Taking a few steps back, Nick moved toward the ball, which was still in the air, reaching his hands out to snatch it and—

A smaller, lithe figure jumped up in front of him, snagging the catch and cradling the ball in her arms as she continued her arch backwards until she slammed full force against him, knocking the air—and his center of gravity—out of him. Nick landed on his back, a throbbing pain in his jaw becoming more pronounced from where her head had slammed on their landing.

Wait. *Their* landing...?

Yep. Anna Blake was now splayed across him, her arm tangled under him and her soft breasts pressed directly against his right shoulder, her other arm clinging to the ball.

Her head bobbed up, and her eyes widened in surprise.

Grapefruit. That was what she smelled like. Vanilla and grapefruit. Fresh and sharp but also sweet and...succulent. Kind of like her.

He blinked. What the hell was wrong with him? That had to be the stupidest thing that had ever crossed his mind. He must have hit his head harder on impact than he thought.

Nick gazed up, aware that the group had gathered

around them. Anna must have become aware of them, too, as she rolled off him and onto the ground.

"You two okay?" Janie asked.

"I'm fine. Just trying to salvage my pride," Anna said, still lying on the ground.

"Nick?" Dax asked.

Nick sat up, rubbing his jaw. "Me, too. Just had the wind knocked out of me is all."

Chris reached his hand out to Anna and pulled her up in one motion. "That a girl! Looks like you need to take a page from this beautiful woman's play list, St. Claire. She just successfully intercepted the ball."

Now that any concerns of real injury were dismissed, a cheer went up among Janie's team. It was hard to miss the smile of satisfaction on Anna's face as she glanced back at him.

He nodded his head in acknowledgment, willing to give credit where it was due.

She'd outmaneuvered him. He could own that.

But he'd be damn sure not to let it happen again.

CHAPTER 5

ANNA BIT her bottom lip as she sank onto the lounge chair a few feet from the pool, where tonight's bridal shower was taking place, the aches and soreness impossible to ignore. They were worth it, however, just to see the look of shock on Nick's face as they'd fallen over.

"I don't know when I've had so much fun. Bruised knees and all," Janie said, coming from out of nowhere and sinking onto the chair beside her.

"Me, too," Anna said in surprise.

Up until the moment she and Nick reached their agreement, Anna had been feeling sick. Sick that she was going to have to befriend people she didn't know, people who probably were already judging her and why she was here now, and, worse, once she got them to trust her and open up to her, betray that trust by selling them out for any dirt she uncovered. Without those worries hanging over her head, she'd finally breathed freely again, making it easier to get into the spirit of the game.

Kicking Nick's butt had been an unexpected bonus. As was finding herself lying on top of him seconds later. It had been one thing to observe the breadth of his chest, the subtle, well-toned biceps of his arms, or his slim hips and stomach; it was another thing entirely to feel those attributes pressed against her when she was lying directly on top of him.

It had taken her breath away more than their moment of impact.

"So, how did you and Dax meet?" Anna asked, needing a diversion.

"This is a good one," Megan said, sinking into the seat on the other side of Janie. Trish and Sara scooted their seats over to join the trio, creating a small circle that now included Anna.

"Dax and I first met at summer camp. I was thirteen, and he was a worldly fourteen years old. Even then I knew he was the guy for me." Janie lifted her wrist to reveal a very threadbare bracelet made of intricate knots. "We exchanged these bracelets. Love bracelets, I called them."

"They were voted cutest couple at the end-of-camp award ceremony," Sara said, smiling at her friend.

"Were you there?" Anna asked the brunette, who, before now, hadn't exchanged more than two words with her.

"She sure was. We've known each other since the third grade. Anyhow, I didn't make it back to the camp the next year," Janie continued. "My mom was going through an early midlife crisis and dragged me to Spain for the entire summer. I had to wait until Sara got back from camp to hear anything about Dax, who, she told me, had been lost without me. The next summer no one made it to camp thanks to a rat infestation that closed the place. After that, we both moved on, chalking up our summer as a brief but memorable childhood romance."

"And you might never have seen poor Dax again had I

not suggested we all go down to Mexico for spring break to celebrate our last year at college," Trish said.

"Very true," Janie said. "Megan and I wanted the Virgin Islands, but Chantelle and Trish wanted Mexico. Sara broke the tie and there you go. We were all sipping our margaritas poolside when who should show up but Dax St. Claire, after all those years. Except instead of a cute fourteen year old, he was insanely hot. Those fluttery butterflies I'd had at thirteen were still there at twenty-two, only better."

"You two were practically attached at the hip after that," Trish said.

"Guilty. And two years later, we're finally going to say I do," Janie finished, her face flushed a pretty pink.

Trish ran to the bar, returning with a tray of martini glasses rimmed with pink sugar and filled with an unknown pink liquid. "I think it's time we got this little party started with a toast. To Janie and Dax, childhood sweethearts who are finally getting their happily ever after."

Anna took one of the glasses and tapped it against the women's around her before taking a sip of the overly sweet but highly potent concoction.

"How about you?" Janie asked, looking directly at Anna.

"Me what?"

"Well, we barely know each other, something that I very much want to rectify," Janie said earnestly. "Was there ever some great love in your life? A childhood romance or maybe a high school sweetheart?"

Right. "Nope. I've always been a woman who likes her independence."

Not to mention the fact that boys never looked at her that way. Romantically. Not that she'd been all that interested in boys back then, either, or at least not most of them. She'd been what her mom had called a late bloomer.

Even in college, when she finally started dating and coming into her own sense of self, Anna had never been interested in getting tied down to anyone, preferring the freedom of being single, like her mom.

"Wait. Never?" Megan asked. "I mean, you've had a boyfriend, I'm sure."

She shrugged. "Not really. Don't get me wrong. I love men. But relationships carry too much baggage. Too many expectations." Not to mention vulnerabilities. "I just want to have fun, kick back, and not take life too seriously. That's what I have my writing for. The real stuff."

"But don't you ever want to get married someday?" Janie asked.

Anna shrugged. "My mom's never been married and she doesn't seem any worse off for it," Anna said, taking another sip of her drink before she remembered that she thought it was utterly disgusting. She set it down on the small table in front of her. "If anything, she's been able to do more things without a husband. Marriage only tethers you down and places unreasonable expectations on the other person," she said, quoting from her mom.

From Janie's crestfallen expression, Anna realized that this anti-marriage sentiment probably wasn't the pep talk that would win her any awards for maid of honor, which was what Nick had negotiated for. She backtracked. "That is, I mean to say, for me. That's just not part of *my* DNA. But I am sure it works out for lots of people. In fact, one of my best friends is about to get engaged this weekend—not that she's aware of it yet. I know that this guy is perfect for her and she is for him, and they're going to have an incredible life, just like I'm sure that Dax is the perfect guy for you."

"You really think so?" Janie asked, looking hopelessly hopeful.

"Of course she does," Sara said and rose to her feet. "As do we all. Now, without further delay, I say it's time so move on to the equally most dreaded and simultaneously anticipated moment we've been waiting for...the games."

Party games. Did people still do this?

"First up, we're going to play a little wedding Pictionary."

Apparently they did. Although, having the attention back on Janie and Dax was better than having it on her and her nonexistent history of romance.

"It's just like the original game," Sara explained. "Only every card has some tie-in to romance and weddings. We'll split into two teams—"

Janie clutched Anna's arm. "I'm with Anna."

Her tone didn't sound like it would brook any argument. The rest of the girls split off easily enough and they got started, Janie at the white board, pen in hand as she tried to draw what looked like...

An egg?

A roar of definitive male laughter from inside the house caught her attention. She stifled a wave of jealousy at knowing the only game the groomsmen were playing was a mean game of Texas Hold'em, or maybe Seven-Card Stud.

Something told her this was going to be a very long night.

CHAPTER 6

"And look at that," Dax said, splaying his hand of cards, a straight flush that trumped Nick's full house and Jake's three of a kind. He pulled in the poker chips from the center of the table and added them to his growing pile. "Thanks again for deciding to raise the stakes for tonight's game, Nick."

"Don't mention it," Nick said, realizing that he'd only done so in the hopes of forcing himself to keep his focus on the game at hand, a ruse that he'd failed at miserably. Particularly when the soft laughter from the bridal shower that was taking place out at the pool kept drawing his attention.

Was Anna keeping up her end of the bargain and playing nicely with the other women as she'd promised? Maybe he should move a little closer to the door to see if he could hear the conversation...

Chris was shuffling the cards when a particular raucous cry of female laughter stopped him and he smiled, turning his gaze to Nick. "So what's the story with you and Anna? Is there something going on between you that I need to know? I'd hate to overwhelm her with my irresistible charm if there is."

"You have nothing to worry about, buddy," Nick said, careful to keep his tone light. "There's nothing between us and never was—other than some bad high school memories."

Chris nodded and resumed his shuffling. Dax, however, studied him. "I don't know, bro. That may have been true in high school, but I can't help but notice a certain...vibe between you."

"Vibe?" Nick snorted before taking a pull from his beer. "Sure, maybe of distrust."

"So that little exchange before today's game was merely you two swearing your undying hatred for each other?" Dax persisted.

"We were coming to an understanding of how we were going to get through this week without killing each other."

"Killing each other?" Jake asked, grinning. "That's not exactly what I was worried about when she dropped you out on the field earlier."

Nick rolled his eyes. "She hardly dropped me. Don't you guys have more interesting things to do than to watch what I'm doing—or rather, not doing—with Dax's future sister-in-law?"

Chris dealt the cards. "All right. We hear you. The lovely Anna Blake is fair game."

"Of course she is," Nick said, even if the thought of this buffoon and the blue-eyed reporter irked him. He finished off his beer. "Actually, I think I'm going to sit this one out and see if I can rustle up something better to drink from the kitchen. You know me. My preferred poison is of the single malt variety."

Nick pushed his cards back to Chris and left the table. As he'd expected, the men barely acknowledged his exit, too caught up in studying their hands to pay him any mind. He relished the blissful silence and emptiness of the large kitchen that was dark, save for the run of lights above the island. He crossed the tiled floor toward the liquor-filled teak sideboard at the other end of the room, where he'd seen someone restock it earlier. After grabbing the desired bottle of Scotch whiskey, he shut the cabinet and looked around for a fresh glass.

Footsteps coming from the hallway alerted him to someone else's arrival. It wasn't difficult to identify the newcomer with the long blonde hair who sauntered in a moment later. She stopped in the middle of the floor, her face turned toward the dim light, her hands balling and un-balling in fists as she muttered something under her breath. She looked sorely in need of a stiff drink, nearly as much as he did.

"You talk to yourself a lot. Do the voices ever answer?" he asked.

She flinched at hearing his voice and whirled around to face him.

"Crap," she said and placed her hand over her heart. "Are you planning on spying on me this entire week?"

"Only as necessary. This meeting, however, is merely a happy coincidence. What are you doing in here, anyway? Shouldn't you be outside enjoying the bridal shower?"

Instead of answering, she walked to the bank of cupboards and started opening and closing them. The short and sexy denim cutoffs she'd been wearing at the park were replaced with a tomato-red spaghetti-strapped dress that was bold and daring, like her. His eyes continued to travel up past her softly curving hips and her narrow waist. The heavy shiny mass of honey-blonde hair fell past her shoul-ders to cover her nearly bare back.

He did a mental headshake at the inappropriate

thoughts running through his head. This was Anna Blake, the woman whose memory would have brought anger, frustration, and distrust before today. The anger and frustration had certainly lessened over the past ten years, but the distrust remained strong.

"One hour and forty-five minutes," Anna said suddenly, and he was thankful she couldn't read his thoughts. "That's how long I've been sitting out there drawing such scintillating pictures as 'catching the bouquet' and 'wedding bell blues.'" She stopped at a cabinet door revealing a shining display of crystal tumblers. Grabbing two, she turned around. "I think that entitles me to something a little stiffer than the pink martinis they're serving outside—and fifteen minutes of your time, as you promised."

From the sounds of laughter that had been rolling in from outside tonight, he had to admit that she appeared to have held up her end of the bargain for today. Nick headed to the breakfast nook, located in the corner of the kitchen. He twisted the cap off the bottle before placing it on the table and taking a seat. "What is it you want to know?"

He poured the whiskey and slid a glass across the table toward her before taking a lingering sip of the heady liquor as he waited.

Anna laid the phone on the table next to her glass. "I assume it's okay if I record our interview."

"I wouldn't want it any other way."

She whirled the fluid around before taking a sip. She grimaced, evidently not enjoying the flavor, but she didn't complain. Instead, she took another drink before returning it to the table and turning those wide eyes on him.

"Okay. Let's start with some easy questions. As everyone knows, you come from a long line of St. Claires who've had their finger in the proverbial political pie. Your dad was a

US senator. Your granddad, a governor decades before that. Have you always wanted to follow in their footsteps?"

He chuckled lightly. "You do realize that that's the same question you asked me almost ten years ago? When we first sat down for our interview during the student election?"

She smiled innocently. "I just wanted to give you the chance to clear up the record. In case maybe your answer has evolved in the past decade."

Nick didn't have to ask what she meant, as he recalled having made some flippant remark about the election being a one-off to him. He didn't want it to seem like he had anything invested in the race on the chance he lost. He'd known even then that Anna hadn't bought it. She'd sensed his ambition and determination.

It was the beginning of their relationship of distrust.

He looked across the table, his gaze stopping at the sight of her left dress strap, no wider than a shoelace, which had fallen off one shoulder. In defiance to the laws of gravity, the top of her dress hadn't slipped down, shored up by the swelling of her full breasts that he'd been trying to pretend didn't exist.

What had she been saying? He pulled his gaze upward.

The chastising look on her face told him she likely knew where his gaze had been and she wasn't surprised. And why would she be? She had to know by now of her considerable appeal to the opposite sex.

Not that she'd been entirely without allure in high school. Sure, she hadn't any of the curves that she wore so confidently now, but she'd had the same pouty lips, the same sass that went with that full mouth, and the same wide blue-gray eyes that were not only pretty but had made him feel like she could see through him, through his carefully honed mask of confidence to the insecurities underneath. It was what had made him almost afraid of her then, but now as a fully grown man who had reached a level of his own maturity, it made him only more curious.

And intrigued.

Nick cleared his throat. "You're right. But as a wildly insecure seventeen-year-old who was afraid you and everyone else could see how desperately I wanted the win, I tried to play it cool, like I didn't care if I won or not. To answer your question, though, yes. I've always known I wanted to enter a life of public service."

"Because of your dad?" she asked.

"He played a large part in that decision, that's for sure. I remember this time, I would have been about eight, and my dad had returned from DC and was meeting with some constituents out of the local office. I was frustrated because we were supposed to have gone to the park to play ball, but he needed to stop in. The way people looked at him, so respectfully, almost...reverently, it made me proud. Whether they were thanking him for his work or giving him grief for not giving the vote they'd wanted, he treated them all like their opinions mattered. I finally could see that what he was doing was making a real difference in these people's lives."

It was another five years before his disillusionment about his dad's greatness came to a screeching halt. But that was a matter that he would never go into, least of all with Anna Blake.

"Years later, when that stroke hit him and he had to give up his seat, we all knew it was only a matter of time. Dad could no longer do what he loved doing, and in the end it... it killed him." Nick swallowed past the lump that rose in his throat whenever he remembered his dad's last few weeks of life.

"I'm sorry," Anna said gently. "That must have been

rough for you. You were at Georgetown at the time, weren't you?"

He gave her an odd look, wondering how much about his life she actually knew. It made him realize how little he knew of her, something he unexplainably wanted to remedy. "Yeah. I took the semester off to be there for him, and for Dax and Mom. When he died, I returned to school, eventually going on to get a master's in public administration. The rest I'm sure you're familiar with."

Running for the city's supervisor position two years ago had turned his life into an open book. What he hadn't volunteered became common knowledge thanks to the bounties that editors like Charlie Kravitz placed on his head. It was a price he was still getting used to and a part of going into public service.

"It was quite the coup at the time. You became the youngest city supervisor in the city's history."

"That's right, but I'll bet that you were voting for the other guy to win."

She smiled, not giving anything away. "Speaking of your current position as a public servant for the city, how exactly are you able to be here instead of back in the city?"

"I'm in contact with my office and keeping abreast of any developments, and my committee isn't scheduled for any votes this week, so there should be little to no effect."

"And your mother? She must be thrilled about the upcoming senatorial campaign," she said, running a finger around the rim of her glass. "I'm betting she's had your entire political career plotted since birth."

She wasn't far off the mark. "You speak as if you know her."

"I know her enough," she muttered under her breath.

That stopped him. "How would you know my mother?"

Anna looked up, studying him suspiciously. "You know how."

He shook his head. "I'm afraid I don't.

"You don't know anything about her campaign to try and get me expelled from school?"

He set his glass down, knowing with cold certainty that he wasn't going to like what he was about to hear. "Was this because of the story you did during the student election?"

"Ding ding ding. Give the gentleman his prize," she said as if trying for humor only to have her joke fall flat. "The day after my story ran, she found me walking home from school and thought it was a good time for us to chat. Naively, I climbed into her town car. Had her driver not been there, I probably would have run, but I thought at least there'd be a witness."

Despite her attempt at humor, he could see her hand trembled as she set her drink back on the table. "What did she say?" he asked softly.

"I don't know. Just stuff. Something about my being a desperate, no-name girl with no future outside of the fast-food industry. And a few other things that I can't remember."

He doubted that. He would bet she remembered every word that his mother had told her and he shuddered at the possibilities. His mother could be unflinchingly harsh.

"It wasn't until I got to school the next morning that I discovered she'd also spoken to Headmaster Higgins and a number of parents on the school board about getting me expelled. When that didn't work, she asked that I be booted off the paper. The entire week was a nightmare, not helped by the fact that my mom was somewhere in Indonesia and I had no way of reaching her. It took until Friday for the headmaster to pull me into his office and assure me that I still had my place on the paper, thanks in large part to some all-powerful benefactor who pulled a few favors. In the end, your mother had to be satisfied with my apology and a retraction in the next edition of the student paper."

"I'm sorry, Anna. I didn't realize she'd done all of that. She did that entirely on her own. Although, if I'm being honest, I probably wouldn't have objected too hard had I known. I was pretty pissed off at you."

She looked down at the counter, playing with her phone. "If we're being honest, I did feel horrible about what happened. I should have double-checked my source, but I let my personal bias where you were concerned get the best of me. I was wrong. And...and I'm sorry. It was a hard lesson to learn. But necessary."

"Wait. Are you actually apologizing to me?"

She met his gaze, holding it. "I am. I was wrong."

He nodded. "Thank you. It's nice to hear." He remembered another thing she mentioned. About her mother. Parrish Hall was a small school with a small student body. As such, most people knew each other, knew who their parents were, usually because the school strongly encouraged parents to participate in school events. And even though Anna was a year his junior, he didn't have any recollection of her mom. "So was your mom gone a lot like that when you were growing up?"

"Every so often. She's a cultural anthropologist, so traveling, staying places for long periods of time were part of the job. My mom's aunt took care of me when she was gone up until she died when I was fourteen. By then I was old enough to handle being alone when she was away."

"How long could she be gone?"

Anna shrugged. "Anywhere from three weeks to three months. But it wasn't like I was completely on my own. She had a circle of friends that I grew up knowing I could reach out to if I needed to."

Nick had thought nothing could be worse than having a mom who was overly involved in your life. The alternative, having one hardly there at all, suddenly seemed worse.

Anna went to take another drink only to find it was gone. Nick didn't hesitate as he topped off her glass and then his own. She held her glass a little too tightly, her fingers white.

He realized one thing that Anna seemed to hate more than him.

Vulnerability.

Whether from a frequently absent mother who couldn't be bothered with the day-to-day events of her daughter's life or a father who had washed his hands of her entirely. It was no wonder she found it difficult to open up to Janie.

"Not that I'm missing her or anything, but I have been curious why your mother hasn't graced the festivities with her presence," Anna said. "Is there any chance she will be joining us? Or is her broomstick out of commission?"

He smiled. "My mother is a surprisingly busy woman these days. She's involved in more political action committees than I can count, not to mention the St. Claire Foundation she heads, so we're all safe to enjoy the frivolity of the week without her presence." Although Kathryn St. Claire had found the time to leave him several lengthy voice mails about ideas she had for his upcoming election and to ask him how things were going with Sara. She still hadn't given up hope on that reconciliation. "Last I heard, she'll be arriving in time for Friday's rehearsal dinner."

"Yay," she said without enthusiasm. "Now that we've covered your family, why don't we move on to something new? The number one question that pops up in the comments whenever we run a story about you is whether or not you are currently involved with anyone romantically." She looked up at him. "Care to comment?"

That was definitely not something he was ready to tackle. Nick looked at his watch, surprised to see that they'd well exceeded their fifteen-minute allotment of time for tonight's interview. He smiled. "Darn. As much as I'd love to go into that with you, it looks like we're out of time."

"Convenient."

"On that note"—he rose, putting the cap back on the bottle—"I probably had better rejoin the men. And you... you should probably see if Janie needs attending to."

She looked so disgruntled he couldn't help but grin. Even disgruntled she was pretty, her face bright with color whether from the commentary exchanged, the alcohol, or something more. Something that he was more than aware of pulsing between them, making him want to stay, to see what more he could uncover about this woman even though the conversation was supposed to have been focused on him.

Which was why it was best that he leave now. Before he leaned forward and skimmed her bare shoulder with his fingertips as he'd been wanting to do this entire time. Before he leaned forward and tested his lips against hers, to see if she tasted like the Scotch in her glass or something sweeter and infinitely more sensuous.

Before he took complete leave of his senses.

CHAPTER 7

LYING on her bed later that night, her phone tucked under her chin, Anna laughed at something her friend Quinn recounted from her day back in the city. Quinn was apparently suffering from momentary loneliness with Anna gone, Tessa visiting her brothers in Sonoma, and her boyfriend, James, flying somewhere over the Midwest.

A soft knock on her door had her pausing. Another knock followed, unmistakable this time.

"Hey, Quinn, I've got to run. If I don't talk to you before, have fun with James this weekend."

"I will, and you try to relax and enjoy yourself."

After saying their good-byes, Anna dropped the phone and hopped off the bed. Grateful she'd worn cutoff sweats, a tank top, and her most comfortable gray hoodie to provide her warmth in these cooler summer nights here in Napa, she crossed the room unworried about modesty as she opened the door.

For a second, the possibility that it was Nick on the other side of the door brought a flurry of nerves.

Only it wasn't Nick. It was Janie, carrying a tray filled

with milk, sodas, bottled waters, and a bag of Chips Ahoy chocolate-chunk cookies. Anna's favorite.

"I thought, if you were up to it, maybe the two of us could have a little tête-à-tête."

The last thing Anna was emotionally ready for was late-night girl talk with her long-lost little sister, but the hope in Janie's eyes, the way she bit her bottom lip nervously made it all but impossible to deny her. "Sure."

Janie's smile lit up her entire being as she flitted past to set the tray on the bed before hopping on. With her hair pulled back and face clean of makeup, she seemed more like a sixteen-year-old at a slumber party than a twenty-four-year-old almost bride. Of course, the pug-covered pajamas didn't help.

"Now be honest. Are you having a good time?" Janie asked.

Anna sat across from her on the bed, taking a moment to consider the question, but before she could reply, Janie's face fell. "You hate it here. Is it the girls? Did someone say something? Or...or is it maybe...me? Did I do something? If all the activities are too much, you don't have to do them. I would understand if you needed more quiet time to yourself..."

"I'm having a wonderful time," she said, rushing in to assure the younger woman. "Better than I thought I would. Honest."

Janie's eyes still appeared uncertain. "You can tell me the truth if you're not. I'll be okay," she said, all evidence to the contrary.

"I'll admit that I'm not the biggest people person, so being surrounded by so many new people twenty-four seven is somewhat challenging, but it hasn't been without its highlights, too."

"Like taking down Nick so gloriously out on the field today?" Janie asked and laughed.

"Yes. Exactly like that." Anna grinned at the memory of Nick's surprised face when he hit the ground.

"Well, you have a couple more days to adjust to us before the next wave hits us. One person you won't have to worry about meeting, however, is our aunt Lenore—Daddy's sister. She's going be here in time for Friday's rehearsal dinner. You're going to love her." Janie ripped open the bag of cookies. "She's lived in London since her last husband died about ten years ago, but she always comes for visits. I don't know what I would have done without her."

Anna was aware of who the woman was. Malcolm's junior by six years, she'd been married twice but had no kids. It was written in the piece the *Chronicle* did when Malcolm died. But that was all she knew.

Janie offered the cookies to Anna before crunching into one. Anna nibbled at hers, even though ordinarily she would have shoved the entire thing in her mouth.

"The holidays were only bearable because of Aunt Lenore," Janie said. "She would always appear and whisk me away on some exciting adventure or another, whether to a water park, where she jumped right in there with me, to Seattle for lunch at the Space Needle, or just hanging out on the beach for the day. I think my favorite memory was when she took us to this little park in Santa Rosa where she let me ride the carousel for as long as I wanted. I was probably only seven or eight and had wanted to spend the whole day there riding around on the back of the most beautiful horse, my head tilted back." She smiled at the memory, and then she shook her head. "I don't know if I ever felt safer and more loved than I did that day, with her waving and smiling at me from the side."

"She sounds great," Anna said, unable to tamp down the sting of envy at her sister's experience with this mysterious woman.

"She is. She also used to slip bags of jelly beans into my coat pockets or the bottom of a box of gifts that she'd brought me. Cotton-candy-flavored were my favorite, but I would have eaten any variety just to get a taste of their sugary goodness. It was all hush hush, though, since my mom was afraid that I'd get fat and had me on a strict diet since I was twelve. No candy, soda, or"—she motioned to the half-eaten morsel in her hand—"cookies for me."

Her mother sounded like a real treat, but Anna restrained herself from saying as much. Instead, she jumped on another question that was surfacing in her mind. One common thread she was picking up in the few conversations she'd had with Janie was a complete absence of any reference to one person. "What about your dad? Where was he during all this?"

Janie's smile wavered. "Oh. Well, Daddy was usually too busy for that kind of stuff. He had the company to run and business contacts to keep up. He traveled a great deal, and when he was around, I usually needed to stay out of the way so he could concentrate. What about you? Was it just you and your mom? She never married or had any other kids?"

"It was always just the two of us." Rachel Blake liked her independence too much to tie herself down to anyone.

Janie nodded and put the other half of the cookie in her mouth. "Well, it was usually just me rambling around alone here, too. Not that I'm complaining, since there was loads to do, between tennis lessons, swimming, and horseback riding. You're not going to believe this, but I always wished for a sister. Someone to play games with when the nanny got too bored or tired. Someone to share my birthday cake with when, more times than not, my parents were away for some reason or another. Even someone to fight with when we both wanted the same bedroom—or whatever silly things sisters fight about. Someone who would...get me, you know? And to think that all that time you were out there, maybe thinking the same thing."

"Who knows? You might have hated me," Anna said. "I was kind of...intense back then. Just ask Nick. I was obsessed with my writing and was always searching for 'the big story.'" She hesitated. Although Anna wasn't about to share all her deepest and darkest wishes and desires just because Janie had done the same, she could reveal a little something of herself. "Truthfully, I didn't really have any friends back then. Most of the kids who went to my school were all about what kind of car people drove, who their family was, and who *they* knew or summered with, and I... well, I didn't really have anything of value to add to the mix. My mom was always the most fascinating person in the world to me, but a semi-nomadic anthropology professor from Berkeley wasn't exactly traveling in the same circles as the Eastwoods or the Coppolas."

"I think your life sounds fascinating. And if none of those kids were willing to take the time to get to know you, that's their loss." Janie took another cookie and pushed the bag away from her. "If I don't stop soon, I might not be able to squeeze into my dress on Saturday.

"Please. You're going to look beautiful."

"You mentioned Nick. What's the story there?"

Anna pretended to be confused. "What do you mean? We went to high school together. That's all."

"Right." Janie shook her head and smiled. "There's obviously some sexual tension whenever you're together. I mean, he can hardly keep his eyes off of you."

Anna snorted. "Right. If Nick's watching me, it's purely a defense mechanism."

"Whatever happened between you two anyhow?"

Well, there was no reason to keep it a secret. She'd find out eventually. Anna relayed the big picture. About the story that she'd written without adequately verifying the source for her information. Of the aftermath with Nick's mother. Of Nick's anger even after the retraction that had them feuding for the rest of the year, with Anna holding him to task for every campaign promise he'd made and Nick following up those stories with long, blistering letters in the editorial pages of the same paper.

This earned Janie's giggles, and now, with the advantage of time, Anna could see the humor in it, too. He'd certainly kept her on her toes and she his.

"Well, whatever your history together, there are definite sparks when you two are together. Sara's practically pea-green with jealousy."

"Yeah. I noticed that," Anna said, choosing to ignore the bit about sparks." What's the story there?"

"I set them up about a year ago, but they were only together for a few months before Nick called it off. I never really understood what happened, despite pestering Dax for the details. Sara has hinted that they might have hooked up again at our engagement party last fall, but I haven't been able to confirm that. But I wouldn't worry about her if I were you," Janie added. "Dax assures me that, at least for Nick, there's nothing there."

"Are you kidding? Why should I care who Nick dates? Nick and I are barely drying the ink on our own tentative truce. Believe me, romance is definitely not on my radar."

"Hmmm," Janie said, but she didn't expand before taking a sip of water. "Hey. Are you tired? Because I'm in the mood to watch a good rom com. Maybe...*When Harry Met Sally*? We could put it on and finish off these cookies, hiding the evidence from my mother."

The movie was one of Anna's all-time favorites. Suddenly she wasn't as tired as she'd thought. "Why not?"

Anna grabbed another cookie, this time shoving the entire thing into her mouth, as Janie squealed and grabbed the remote to the television to set up their screening.

Okay, so maybe hanging out with her sister wasn't as bad as she'd thought.

Another image came to mind of a person who wasn't as bad as she'd thought. Of a guy who had been at the heart of a painfully excruciating year. A guy who she could now see was maybe not the villain in the story that she'd painted him to be.

A guy who maybe was worth giving a chance. At least at being a friend.

CHAPTER 8

NICK SLOWED his pace as he rounded the corner of the estate's tennis court as he took his morning run, his thoughts still on last night's brief but enlightening interlude with the nosy reporter.

He'd entered their agreement carrying a certain opinion about Anna as a self-centered, egotistical bloodsucker who had the power to crush his brother's vision of the perfect week, a power that he had to curtail. But in the space of one conversation, he was beginning to rethink that original opinion. Their conversation gave him a different perspective of the woman he'd cursed for years.

Unlike Nick, who'd grown up secure in knowing both of his parents loved and supported him in all of his endeavors, Anna had grown up without her father's love or support or even his acknowledgment that she was his daughter. Although Anna had given her mother an excuse for not being more present in her life, her actions of putting her career before her daughter couldn't have gone unnoticed.

The people she should have been able to count on as a kid had been absent. Nick could understand why Anna's writing had become so paramount in her life. It was the only thing she had.

Until now, that was.

He smiled. Whether Anna was aware of it or not, Janie Van Hollins was a forcible person, and when she wanted something, she wouldn't stop until she had it. She definitely wanted a relationship with Anna. Anna just had to let her defenses down and allow it to happen.

He slowed his pace. Wasn't that what Sara had asked of him when she tried to get back together last fall? To let her in?

Immediately he dismissed that notion. With Sara, it had been completely different. His issue wasn't letting people in. He could let them in. His problem was trusting those people not to have some ulterior motive.

Up ahead, he noticed some movement. Another person came into sight, a runner with a bouncy blonde ponytail and long, lean legs, also lost in thought. She seemed unaware he was coming up behind her.

Unobserved, he took a moment to check out the strength in her legs, the lean curves of her hips, and the small, taut waist.

No. Nick pulled his gaze away, needing to get a grip. He wasn't here to kindle a romance with anyone, especially not a smart-mouthed reporter. He had too many other things on his plate, not the least of which was his own campaign he needed to be focusing on from now until he gave that acceptance speech.

Nick settled on staring at the back of her neck, somewhere that should have been safe. Nope. Not any better. The only solution would be to ease past her and put her in his rear view.

Picking up the pace, Nick was about to round up on her

when her head turned in his direction. Instead of shock or a momentary loss of momentum, she curled her lips into a smile of determination and dug in harder, sprinting ahead.

So that was how she wanted to play.

Nick enjoyed a good challenge, especially when he saw that he was matched with such a formidable foe, and he increased his speed until he was alongside her. She didn't bother to look over at him again, instead focusing on the path ahead.

They continued at this rate, her breathing down his neck and refusing to give an inch, until his legs were burning and his chest was heaving painfully. He wasn't used to being pushed so hard, and he had to admit he liked it.

"Ready to call it?" he asked, hearing her breath becoming just as labored, her pace slowing ever so slightly.

"Never."

He almost laughed, knowing that she was exhausted and probably close to breaking but not willing to give him an inch. "How about we race to the fountain at the courtyard?"

"You're on."

Whatever weakness he thought he'd perceived in her stride immediately disappeared as she pushed herself ahead of him. He wondered briefly whether he'd been played, but was too late, because with that sudden unseen burst, she'd put herself enough in the lead in those last few seconds, and it was over.

She'd won.

Instead of feeling indignant at being played, though, he was relieved that it was over. His lungs burning as much as his legs, he slowed down to catch his breath before collapsing in a pile on the ground.

A second later, Anna dropped next to him, her face bright and pink from the exertion, a bead of sweat trickling down her neck and disappearing into the top of her sports bra, an area that he hadn't been able to admire previously. He swallowed hard at the view of the tantalizing amount of skin above it—and the ample amount hidden from sight.

"You certainly have a singular mind," Anna said.

He glanced up, aware in his oxygen-depleted state of mind that he'd been caught gaping, but instead of appearing disgusted or angry, Anna only rolled her eyes.

"I'm nothing if not consistent."

He stretched forward over his right leg, feeling the pull in his hamstring as Anna did the same. For his own sanity, he kept his eyes on the top of his shoe instead of the view of her more alluring assets.

"That's twice now I've kicked your butt. Not that I'm counting," she boasted, switching legs.

"All a matter of perspective." He sat up and crossed an arm in front of him, lengthening the muscles in his shoulder. "I seem to recall kicking yours with my finely tuned dance steps."

"Okay, that's fair. So one point for you and your ballroom dancing techniques and two points for me and my naturally given athletic prowess at both football and running. Maybe if there's a cooking class later today, you can earn yourself another point. Or you can show me up by darning some socks or sewing a button on your apron?" She looked up from where she'd been leaning forward into a stretch and grinned.

Damn. She was sexy.

Not just because the fullness of her breasts was heard to miss as she leaned toward him. No, her sexiness was deeper. Having to do with the confidence she carried in her every movement. In the way her eyes shined and her lips curved as she smiled at him.

In her ability to challenge him and push herself without fear of failure.

"Hey, I'm all right with that. I'm nothing if not in touch with my feminine side." In fact, her ribbing him about his feminine skills only made him like her—crazily enough— even more. It was definitely a first for him, having someone not vying for his attention. "My mother wouldn't have it any other way. After all, women make up fifty percent of my constituents."

"Ah. That's right. Always the angle."

A jingling beat from Anna's phone rang out. "Crap. That's my reminder for breakfast. Janie wanted everyone to have a full meal before this morning's dance lesson and before we head out for the winery tour. The last thing she wants is people passing out drunk after the first winery visit of the day."

"Full meal or not, a winery tour with a group like this is always asking for disaster. Mark my words. Someone will be three sheets to the wind by lunch."

Anna came to her feet easily, already recovered, and gave him a funny look. "Three sheets to the wind? What are you, ninety?"

Not one to be shown up, Nick hopped to his own feet. "Voters in the fifty-five-and-over demographic are my highest-voting constituents. Not to mention the older ladies love me."

She rolled her eyes. "Of course they do."

He eyed the terrace doors and looked back at her, lifting his brows in a challenge.

"You really want to race again? Hasn't your ego taken enough of a blow?" she asked.

"Not any more than—" But whatever words he was going to say next were lost in the wind when Anna darted forward, not waiting for the signal as she took off in a sprint.

He didn't even have a chance.

ANNA SIPPED the fragrant red wine—the third glass set before each member of their party—trying to remember the instructions about savoring the flavors, doing something with the tongue...

Eh. She gulped her swallow down. She was hopeless.

Looking around, she noticed a few of the others doing it the "proper" way, their mouths pursed as if they knew what they were doing. It wasn't that Anna didn't have an appreciation for good wine. Tessa's family owned a small vineyard in the Sonoma area, and in the past few years, she'd brought her love for wine to her two roommates. Tessa could probably tell her every note in the wine's bouquet without hesitation while Anna could only tell if she liked it or not—no need to dissect further.

From over the rim of her glass, she spied Nick tossing his back, barely swishing it in his mouth per the instructions, as he nodded at whatever Jake and Megan were saying. He was freshly showered and shaven since this morning's run, and his short dark hair still appeared damp where it waved back from his forehead, giving him an almost boyish look.

As if unaware of her attention, Nick continued his discussion, pausing after a moment to lick some invisible droplet of wine off his full bottom lip. A quiver of desire thrummed through her, and she was envious for a moment of his tongue and his lips and—

Holy Hannah.

If she knew what was good for her, she'd look away,

maybe to Janie and Dax a few seats away, where they were being adorable as usual while they smiled and whispered, their heads bent over the other. Only...

Nick was wearing a light-gray crew neck tee that outlined every line and bulge on that taut torso—telling her he did more than just run to stay in such crazy shape—and faded black jeans that weren't too baggy or too tight, offering just the right amount of give and grab to keep a girl's attention.

Almost unbidden, she remembered this morning's run and the rush of adrenaline brought on as much by the physical high of racing as the high of being in the presence of an incredibly sexy guy with dark brown eyes that practically smoldered as he gazed at her. A gaze that she almost wished would turn her way again.

It was silly. And stupid. Yes, there was definitely a strong physical attraction between them, one that, if he were anyone else, she would have acted on if only to get him out of her system.

But this was Nick St. Claire and there was nothing ordinary about him.

"What do you think?" Chris asked from next to her, drawing her back to the present. "Being honest, they all kind of taste the same to me."

"I'm right with you."

Now Chris, on the other hand, had no baggage that would present a problem if they decided to move their flirtation up a notch. With this guy, what you saw was what you got—an entertaining week with laughter, playful exchanges, no-strings-attached kisses, and maybe a little bit more before they both said their good-byes and moved on with their separate lives.

Chris was who she should be throwing energy toward,

instead of sitting there thinking about the brooding guy at the other end of the counter who was nothing but trouble.

It looked like she wasn't the only one who had eyes for Nick. Sara crossed over to Nick and slipped onto the stool next to him, laying her hand possessively on his arm, like she'd done it a million times before. Nick didn't remove it, and Anna fought an irrational sense of jealousy at the sight of the two of them. Sure, Janie had said things were over between him and Sara, but Janie also said that things had been over between them before, when Nick might or might not have fallen back into her bed.

Just went to show how fickle men could be. Not that it mattered to her either way. He was merely the subject of her story, a story she wanted to get right. That's all.

Her phone vibrated next to her. Leaning over, she caught the caller ID.

"I've got to take this," she said in apology to Chris as she grabbed it and headed out the door. "Charlie. Hey," she said almost breathlessly.

Whatever the woman wanted, calling her in the middle of the day couldn't be good.

"Glad to see you still remember me. It's Thursday afternoon and despite having had two days to dig up something of interest for me, you've gone radio silent."

"Sorry. I actually have a great story that I'm running with and I wanted to tell you sooner, but there's just been a lot of things going on."

"Really? Care to enlighten me?"

"Nick St. Claire has some big news that he's been kind enough to give me an exclusive on. The thing is, he wants to keep it on the down low until after the wedding on Saturday. But I guarantee, Charlie, it's going to be worth it. I've already been interviewing him and should have something finalized and ready to send you by Saturday night."

"That's well and good, Anna, but as your editor, I need a little more. What is the big news?"

Anna remembered Nick's warning that the news of his candidacy had to stay under wraps until after Saturday since he didn't want anything to upstage the wedding. Would Charlie respect that request and keep it quiet if she knew she was sitting on what might be the biggest story *The Rundown* had reported this year?

Anna wasn't willing to take any bets.

"It's just that I...I promised. In exchange for the exclusive, I can't breath a word about it until after the ceremony. But I promise, come Saturday night, I'll have the story wrapped and emailed to you."

There was a long pause before Charlie heaved a sigh. "Fine. You have until ten p.m. Saturday night, not a minute later, to have that story emailed to me or you can start looking for a new job come Sunday."

The line went dead before Anna could respond, and she stood there holding the phone to her chest another minute.

For a second, she had a moment's panic when she thought of all the ways this could go wrong. Nick could be planning on screwing her over so that one of their competitors got the exclusive out there before she'd even submitted it to Charlie. Worse, her hunch he was the guy set to announce his candidacy had been wrong and he'd played her, waiting until the last minute to tell her of his con. Leaving her with nothing.

Waiting for this story, for Nick, was forcing her to run on a lot of faith.

Something she didn't ordinarily have a lot of.

CHAPTER 9

NICK HAD PRETENDED NOT to notice Sara's hand on his arm, determined to keep his attention on his discussion with Jake and Megan. But the weight of it, the possessiveness it invoked, was getting on his nerves.

She waited until Jake and Megan were distracted by a question Trish asked them to lean in. "I couldn't help but notice that your feelings toward the maid of honor seem to have thawed if this morning's dance lessons were any indication."

It was something he'd noticed himself when, instead of looking for ways to throw Anna off balance, he had worked with the woman to improve her skills on the floor. And by the end of the lesson, he had been surprised with how much he'd enjoyed it, something that was easier to do when his partner wasn't wishing a thousand deaths upon him, as she had been yesterday.

"We're simply making the best of the situation. How about you? It seems that you and Chris"—he nodded toward the guy who'd been cozying up to Anna a moment

ago and was now alone and edging closer to Dax and Janie
—"were looking pretty chummy, too."

Where had Anna gone?

"And how did that make you feel, Nick? A little jealous?"

Hardly. In fact, it had been a relief to think that maybe
he could pawn off the woman to someone else for his own
sanity. "Not at all. I'll be happy for you if you find that
special someone who can make all your dreams come true.
Whatever they might be."

"Chris and me? Are you kidding? My taste is a little
more...refined."

"No one said you had to marry the guy, Sara. And you
might find that hanging out with him, with no agenda other
than having fun, could be a welcome change of pace."

"I was hoping you'd be that person."

Patience. He needed patience. Why was he still going
through the motions with her on this issue? "You know
that's not going to happen, Sara. Everyone knows."

"Your mother doesn't know. She called me this morning
to find out if Daddy was still heading his committee on
water rights."

Good God. Why was she asking Sara about that? She
hadn't shared the news about his upcoming announcement,
had she? Damn. He'd avoided his mother's calls the past two
days, something that, in hindsight, had been a mistake. "Did
she tell you why she wanted to know?"

"No. I think she just wants you and me to look past our
differences and try and make this work."

"She's going to have to get used to disappointment then."

He looked over in time to see Dax answer his phone, his
smiling face dissolving into a look of tight concern. As if
knowing Nick was watching him, Dax raised his gaze to his
brother and a look of understanding passed between them.

"Actually, Sara, it looks like Dax might need me. If you'll excuse me."

"Of course. Help Dax. Let me know if you need anything."

Nick nodded and was happy to finally shake off the woman's hand as he followed his brother. Ahead of them, just coming back inside the room, was Anna, her cell phone in hand.

"Good. I was actually hoping to speak with both of you," Dax said to Anna, who looked as confused as he did as they stared at Dax, waiting for him to explain. "I need to ask a massive favor. Our wedding planner just called. Apparently a pipe burst at the restaurant where we are having our rehearsal dinner tomorrow night and it's flooded. Leaving us without a place to have our rehearsal dinner. Lynette is pulling together a short list of possible alternatives, but what with all the other wedding duties and fires she's already handling, she can't investigate them herself. So... I was hoping I could rely on you two to help me out."

"Of course. What do you need?" Nick asked without hesitation.

"Would you two be willing to check out these places for me? It needs to be someplace amazing—or as amazing as possible under these circumstances—since both of our families and friends are going to be there. If it's horrible, it's going to set the wrong tone for the whole wedding and Janie will be devastated."

"No problem," Nick asserted again. "But I am more than capable of doing this by myself, Dax. There's no need to pull Anna from the festivities."

"Maybe, but sometimes I think you look at things too practically and what I need now is something...magical. Something that a female perspective can bring out, and since Anna is Janie's sister and graciously accepted the role of maid of honor, I was hoping she'd be willing to go a little bit further in helping out," Dax said, looking directly at Anna.

"I would be happy to help," Anna said. "This needs to be the opening act for the big day and nothing second-best will do."

For her part, Anna's exuberance seemed sincere, probably because there were two more wineries, a picnic lunch, and game of bocci on the agenda that she wanted to skip. Nick would know since he was of the same mind.

Dax smiled in relief. "I can't tell you both how much this means to me. I know I can trust you two."

Nick already had an app open on his phone, requesting an Uber driver that would get them back to the Van Hollins estate and his car. "You enjoy the afternoon. If Janie wonders where we are, you can say we're cooking up a surprise."

"I will. Thanks again," Dax said and hurried back to the group.

Nick looked at Anna, uncertain of what to say.

Like it or not, he and Anna were going to be stuck together in closer quarters than they'd originally thought.

And hell if that didn't send a ripple of excitement through him.

ANNA LOOKED out the car window, the beauty of the patch-work of row upon row of grapevines laid out against the rolling hills not lost on her. Nor was the enigmatic presence of the man next to her.

They hadn't spoken much on the ride back to the Van

Hollinses' simply because their talkative Uber driver made conversation unnecessary. But now, five minutes out and alone in Nick's black Lexus sedan, the silence was getting oppressive.

The music playing was something of a surprise. She would have pegged him for Mozart or something more mainstream, like Ed Sheeran. Instead, she heard the sexy bluesy vocals of Dylan Charles, a guy who'd gotten his start in San Francisco almost ten years before.

As if he'd read her thoughts, Nick asked, "The music okay?"

"I love Dylan Charles, and this is, in my opinion, his best album." The last album he'd dropped had critics and fans alike balking at the too mainstream, almost pop-like feel. Hopefully, he could rebound and get back to what made him so good.

She studied her phone, where the addresses of the three restaurants that Lynette had sent them were displayed. Two of them were within walking distance from each other, and where they were heading first, saving the last only if necessary since it was farther out of town.

"I didn't get a chance to say this before, but thanks for agreeing to do this," Nick said, glancing over at her. "I'm sure that Dax feels more at ease knowing we're both on it."

"No problem. Besides, there's only so much 'Kumbaya' togetherness I can take. I was afraid that Janie was going to lead everyone in a sing-along on the bus ride to the next stop."

He smiled, the skin around the corners of his eyes crinkling slightly. "Yeah. I wouldn't have put it past her."

"It probably puts a cramp in your plans, though. It seemed like you had some work you were trying to do on the bus earlier," she said, referencing the fact he'd sat alone at the back of the shuttle bus the entire morning, typing like a maniac, only looking up on occasion to scowl at everyone when they got too loud.

"Just email that needed to be sorted. Everything else can wait until later. I'll confess, I'm relieved to have this reprieve from the daylong groupfest."

She chuckled. "I'll just bet. I noticed Sara didn't look very happy to see our departure."

"No? Well, I'm sure she'll find something to distract her. Chris didn't seem that happy to see you go either. What's going on between you two?"

"I like how you did that. Deflected my question about you and Sara to me and Chris."

"It's what I do," he said and grinned unabashedly. "I should warn you, though. About Chris. He's something of a player, so you might want to watch yourself there. Sure, he's friendly and funny and easily the life of any party, but he's not into any kind of commitment. He's too ambitious for that."

She laughed. "You just described almost every guy I've dated, which is why they're perfect for me. I'm not looking for a lifelong commitment either. No happily-ever-after, until-death-do-us-part forever and ever. Blah, blah, blah. Living in the moment is more my style."

"That's kind of cynical. Even for you."

"Just practical. And what about you? I don't see any wifey by your side. Isn't that required for a guy with high political aspirations? Your own Jackie O., someone beautiful, rich, and with all the right connections? Someone like, say...Sara?"

"Not even close," he said, an edge to his tone.

She studied him. "She seems to have everything you would want."

"My mother seems to think so, too. I, however, don't care if she's the 'right' woman on paper. That kind of thing doesn't matter to me."

"What kind of things do matter to you?"

He glanced over again. "Off the record?"

She sighed. "If you insist, but believe me, this is the kind of stuff people want to know."

"Then they'll have to get used to bitter disappointment." He stopped, as if thinking about her question. "I don't really have a type or a list of things I want. I guess I'd like someone who's attractive, of course. Someone who I can hold an intelligent conversation with, who has the same interests as I do, and who, most importantly, is someone I can trust."

It was hard to miss the implication. "You didn't trust Sara?"

"No," he said curtly.

"Oh, come on. You've got to do better than that. I mean, you already know about my tragic family background. It's only fair you tell me something semi-interesting. How about I guess, and you tell me if I'm warm." When he didn't answer, she pushed on. "Was she unfaithful to you?"

"*That* wasn't an issue."

He said it with such confidence she almost rolled her eyes again. Typical male ego.

"All right. Then help me out."

"Well, during the months we were together, it was hard not to notice a sudden upswing in the amount of media coverage of us and our relationship. Coverage that included details about our relationship that they had no business knowing."

Anna recalled her editor's top ten list of celebrities and public figures hanging on her wall. Nick and the St. Claires had never failed to appear. "You've always been an easy target for those kinds of stories, though. Why was this any different?"

They'd reached a light and Nick took a moment to stretch his arms out. "It got to the point where we'd leave for dinner or a movie and the press would already be there waiting, as if someone had tipped them off. Then there was the deluge of personal stories, not just about me but my mom and brother, even issues with my co-op, that no one should have known about." The light turned green and he pulled out again. "Once we ended things, the absence of those same reporters and stories made the truth more obvious."

Could he have been right? Had Sara been leaking that stuff to draw more attention to them? If so, that kind of betrayal from someone you were getting close to, maybe even falling in love with, would have been tough.

"Don't look at me so woefully," Nick said. "It's not like I'm not used to seeing me or my family plastered across the tabloids. You get used to it. It's getting used to the betrayal from people you thought you could trust, the people you thought were your friends or maybe something more, that takes getting used to."

He spoke like this had happened more than one time in his life.

"So if you thought that Sara had betrayed you, why did you risk getting tangled up with her again last fall?" It had been a risk bringing this up, but she had to admit to being more than idly curious about this.

"How the hell are you hearing all of this?" With one hand still on the wheel, he ran his other hand through his hair. "Not that it's your business—wow, that's something I find myself saying a lot around you—but no, I didn't sleep with Sara after the engagement party, contrary to any reports you may have heard."

For some reason, that pleased Anna more than it should. "That list of things you're looking for in a partner... I noticed a few things were absent."

"No. I think it covered everything that I'm looking for."

"You kind of missed two important things." He glanced over to her, his expression curious. "You know? Love? You didn't mention someone you loved. I imagine that would be high up on most people's list."

"Well, it just goes without saying that my wife and I will love each other. I'm not talking about the fireworks-in-the-sky, blow-your-socks-off, I-can't-live-without-you kinds of love. Those things dim with time and leave you with nothing. I'm talking about the slow burn, the love that builds over time, built on mutual respect and—"

Anna feigned a loud yawn. "You're kidding me, right? I mean, that's the whole reason to be with another person. For that whole *bam*. Fireworks moment. When you can't catch your breath and you almost feel like you're free-falling, but in a good way."

"To each his own, I guess," he said and shrugged. "My parents were married for more than thirty years and they lasted that long because they weren't disillusioned about what marriage meant. They knew it wasn't flowers and poetry every day but a matter of being there even when you might not like each other very much."

It sounded pretty sad to her. Sure, she didn't have marriage on her radar, but that didn't mean that she didn't enjoy those moments when she first met a guy she liked and got caught up in the rush of feelings for each other. Of course, for her, when things got too intense, too dramatic, it was time to bail, but that didn't mean she wasn't looking for the next rush with the next guy. The thrill of doing it all again. "And that's what you want then for yourself? Your parents' marriage?"

His jaw tightened and he struggled for a minute. "I didn't say that. But they did give me some perspective of what marriage could be like so I didn't have unrealistic expectations."

That was cryptic and there was definitely more she wanted to ask him, but from the tight grip he had on the steering column, she decided not to push him. At least not right now.

They were quiet again and Anna looked outside at the view.

"What was the other thing?" Nick asked suddenly. She looked at him, confused for a moment. "You said that I missed two things on my list of things I'd like in a partner, in a wife. What was the second?"

She smiled, not needing to remember what it was. It was probably number one on her list. "Fun. You didn't mention someone you can have fun with. Someone who can make you laugh, who can bring you joy, who can make you wonder what new and exciting things might be in store to explore with them that day and every day you're with them."

Nick nodded but didn't ask anything more. "We're here," he said a minute later, sounding relieved as he pulled into a parking spot.

She met him on the sidewalk, enjoying the warm sun on her face and the light, fragrant breeze that carried the smell of freshly baked dough from the doughnut shop they'd parked in front of. They walked along the line of quaint shops selling a variety of overpriced art, knickknacks, and clothing, dodging other tourists who were snapping photos and taking selfies as they took in the small, idyllic Napa town.

Nick stopped and looked up. "This is it."

"It's..." Anna began, not able to find words to finish the sentence as she walked in, Nick behind her.

The place was definitely quaint. Quaint and rustic. Heavy on the rustic. Perfect if you were hosting a lumber-jack breakfast, but not so much if you wanted an elegant dinner for thirty close friends and family.

She raised her brows as Nick leaned down to whisper, "I don't know if this is exactly the magic Dax was looking for."

After they explained why they were there, the hostess, who had already made the arrangements with Lynette to show them around, led the way to their private dining room.

Nick placed his hand at the small of her back, guiding her gently as they followed behind, the confident splay of his fingertips across her back making her all too aware of their strength and warmth.

An innocent gesture. Probably something he hadn't even given a second thought to. But the feelings the touch evoked were anything but innocent.

Magical might have been another word.

CHAPTER 10

MORE THAN AN HOUR LATER, Nick parked the car on the north side of the building and looked over at Anna. "Ready?'

"As ready as I will be under the circumstances. Let's just hope for a miracle," she said and climbed out. Having already walked through the previous locations and sampled from the menus, they were now on to the final option and fast running out of steam.

It wasn't that the last places were terrible or that Napa was scarce on beautiful, elegant, and undoubtedly delicious places to eat. The problem was finding those features along with a generous private dining area to seat around thirty guests with barely more than twenty-four hours to spare in a town where everything was previously booked weeks—if not months—ago.

Yet, despite the seemingly impossible task they'd been finagled into undertaking, he was finding that being stuck with the maid of honor was actually tolerable. Okay, so maybe more than tolerable. Who knew that Anna Blake, girl reporter, could be warm, witty, and charming when she wasn't trying to decimate him?

She also had a way of smiling at him, her eyes sparkling, her head tilted just so, that had his complete attention. Then there was the way the olive color of that short tank-style dress complemented her honey hair and sun-kissed skin and hugged her curves and showed off her great legs. She was the full package.

Well, except for the fact that she had been his sworn enemy for so long, and he didn't know if he could trust her not to screw him over again for the sake of her story—and securing her next byline.

Nick looked around. "The place is nice. Lots of parking and a great view."

The place was also one of the many around Napa boasting the garden-to-table way of running its restaurant that was so popular these days, which probably explained why it was located farther out of town.

"You'd be hard-pressed to find somewhere in this area that wasn't beautiful," Anna said, heading toward the entrance.

"I don't know about you, but I'm getting pretty hungry," Nick said, holding the door open for her. "What do you say we actually get a table and enjoy lunch once we're done?"

"I could definitely eat."

"You're in just the right place then," an older man said in a heavily accented voice that sounded Italian. Nick placed the short, heavyset guy somewhere in his sixties. "I'm Lorenzo. Welcome to my establishment. Will it be just you two?"

"Actually, you're probably expecting us," Anna said. "Lynette was going to call ahead to make arrangements for us to have the tour?"

"Ah, yes. For the rehearsal dinner."

"Yes. But after the tour, we would love to stay and have lunch."

"Of course. Right this way," Lorenzo said, sidling up to Anna as they walked through the main room.

The guy was animated as he showed them the dining room, a bright and airy room with lots of windows that offered similar views outside at the landscape. He led them out to the patio, which, although too small for the numbers they had for the dinner, was charming and, as he explained, could be made available as another space for serving drinks. He took a few minutes to proudly take them out to the garden area to see and appreciate where their produce selection came from.

When the tour was over, Lorenzo escorted them back to the patio and handed them menus. "You're a lucky man, *signore*," he said and smiled at Nick, "to have found someone as perfect as this *angelo*."

Anna grinned impishly and tilted her head. "You hear that? I'm an angel." She laughed and turned back to Lorenzo. "Actually, it's my sister who's getting married. We're here strictly to do our duties as the maid of honor and best man."

"Maybe then someday, eh?" he asked, grinning at them both. "Then you can return and we can help you, too. In the meantime, take your time. I'll get Gina to assist you with your meal."

Anna watched him go, waiting until he was out of earshot to lean forward, a grin on her face. "I can't tell. Do you think that's a legit accent?"

"I was wondering the same thing. When he was talking about his tomatoes, his guard came down, and I swear, for just a minute, the accent slipped."

Anna's eyes were bright with humor. "Well, even if it is

just an act, he gets an A for effort." She paused, looking around, and sighed.

"What is it? You don't like the place?"

"No, it's not that. I like it fine. More than fine. The dining room is big and open and will make a beautiful venue for the dinner. It's just not as special as I would have liked it to be. It's going to feel very similar to the reception. I was hoping there would be something...more. Different but memorable."

"I agree, but of the selection we've seen, this place is probably the best."

She nodded as their server, who introduced herself as Gina, Lorenzo's granddaughter, arrived with a loaf of warm, crusty bread and a complimentary bottle of wine and took their orders.

Once they were alone, Anna picked up her glass, taking a sip of the deep red. "That's delicious. Now don't ask me what the low or high notes were or any of that because I'll just be making stuff up, but I can tell you I would definitely take another glass."

"That's all I need to know," he said and took a drink. "So, are you having any regrets about missing out on the group festivities yet?"

"Far from it. This"—she looked around as the breeze swept a piece of hair across her face—"is more my element."

Nick picked up a knife and sliced the aromatic bread, placing a piece on each of the small plates in front of them. Now that there was a truce between them, there were so many more things he wanted to know about this woman.

He buttered the bread. "You seem to know my entire resume and I realize I barely know anything about you other than you're at a job that seriously undervalues you but the market is tight and you don't have a lot of options. What about college? Where did you go?"

"UC Berkeley." She bit into the bread, nodding as if in approval. "You've got to try this."

He did, agreeing with her assessment. "Berkeley is very impressive. And you mentioned roommates. Tell me about them."

She took a moment to chew and swallow before answering. "Well, after living two long, miserable years in campus housing with roommates from hell, I decided to get an apartment off campus. Only, my budget was severely limited, so I put an ad out for a roommate and was beyond fortunate when Quinn answered it. When we graduated, things weren't looking any better for me on the job front, and with Quinn starting law school, we were more than happy to stick together even as our lease was expiring. While we were looking for a new place, Quinn met Tessa in torts class and we decided to extend our duo to a trio. It's been the best decision I've ever made. They're my girls. Girls, roommates, friends, sisters. They keep me sane."

"And now that you have that money from Malcolm, are you thinking about moving out? Finding your own place? I mean, there must be a lot of opportunities open to you now."

She'd been drinking her water but stopped as she stared at him in disbelief. "You're kidding, right? You don't seriously think I would touch a dime of that money, do you?"

"I don't see why not. You're his daughter. It's the least he could have done for you. From the look you're giving me, I take it you don't agree."

"Definitely not. When I was a kid, it took me a while to figure out how my mom could afford to send me to pricey private schools even though, more times than not, we were eating peanut butter sandwiches and crackers for dinner. She came clean when I was fourteen, admitting that it was because Malcolm had paid for it. It was part of some agreement they'd made when they split that he could cover the cost of the finest education for me, at my mom's insistence. I didn't have much choice in accepting it then, but I do have a choice in accepting his money now. And I'm not interested."

He nodded. "Fair enough. So what will you do with the inheritance?"

"I haven't decided yet, but my plan is to find a worthy charity to donate it to by Christmas."

He wasn't sure if he admired her for her integrity or considered her a fool for not taking the opportunity to reap some of the benefits she'd missed as a kid.

Their food arrived, large plates filled with aromatic and brightly colored vegetables and broiled, seasoned tilapia that had his mouth watering. He watched for a moment as Anna dived in, not trying to hide her appreciation for the delicious food.

He smiled and stabbed a roasted sweet potato. "You know, even though you were the biggest pain in my ass ten years ago, I do wonder, had we met under different circumstances, whether we would have been friends."

She pulled a face and shook her head. "Not a chance."

"What? You don't think I would have met your high standards for friendship?"

"More like I would never have been cool enough to reach even the lower echelons of your social circles."

It was something he couldn't really disagree with. He'd been a jerk back then. He was too conceited and too full of himself. "Well, it's a shame that we didn't. You know, as much as I hated you back then for what I thought was an unfair personal attack, you certainly kept me on my toes."

He smiled, no longer bitter about what had happened. "I'd thought I was going to skate through that election. Until you. You made me step up my game, something I can appreciate in today's political landscape."

"You're welcome?" she said like a question, smiling. She took a bite of tilapia, washing it down with water before speaking. "Being friends would have been a tall order for me back then, too. I completely detested you."

"Yeah, I remember. Why was that exactly?"

This time she lifted her wineglass and drank, skirting her gaze away from him like she was hiding something.

"What? What don't you want to tell me?" he asked, now insanely curious.

"You probably don't even remember."

"Remind me."

"All right. I guess it's fair that I share it with you. It was the moment that fueled my long-standing grudge against you, which ultimately led to the whole cheating story debacle."

She actually had a moment? Something about that didn't bode well for him.

"My first week of freshman year, you and a few other guys were playing that wonderful game of rating the new girls. Apparently, if I'm recalling correctly, you rated me as a two. Out of ten. Let's see...I had the body of a boy, a smile brighter than aluminum foil—that would have been my braces—and I was overall just plain...weird. The *weird* part kind of caught on with your clique, as you might remember. I became the *weird girl*, later elaborated to the weird reporter chick."

Nick could only stare at her in horror. He didn't recall the day in question, but it rang true as something he and his buddies would do.

Anna laughed and took a drink of her wine, her voice strained. "Weird. It seemed like an innocent word on its own. But when you're fifteen and struggling with insecurities about not being good enough—especially for your own father—it felt pretty painful."

He leaned forward. "Hell, Anna, I don't remember saying any of that, but I also know enough about what I was like back then to know your memory is undoubtedly true. I wish more than anything I could take it back. They were stupid words from a cocky, selfish kid who had a hard time seeing outside his small, narrow-minded life. It's a little late, but I am truly sorry. No wonder you hated me with the fire of a thousand suns. I would have, too."

"It wasn't really that big of a deal," she said, pushing her food around on her plate with the fork, still not meeting his eye. "You probably said nothing more than what other people were saying, and I had thin skin back then that I had to toughen up. When I look back now, it's more amusing than anything."

"Anna." He waited for her to look up, her expression guarded. He hated that he'd caused her one minute of pain, not to mention a decade's worth. "No one deserves to be spoken about like that. I have no excuse other than that I was a jerk and deserve your contempt. When I remember the kid you were back then, the word *weird* doesn't come to mind at all. Yes, you were a little awkward, as most everyone was at that age, but you were also fiery, spirited, witty, and, yes, even cute. The only reason you didn't have a line of boys after you wasn't because they thought you were weird, but because you terrified them with your persistence. Boys can be...insecure. We need a hefty dose of adoration from the girls we like, not the blunt truth. Although, if I'd had any brains, I would have welcomed the challenge."

She didn't say anything, and it seemed like she was in shock as her mouth dropped open the slightest bit. Just as quickly, she recovered, smiling at him in a way that had his chest tightening. "Terrifying, huh? And do you still find me terrifying?"

"Absolutely. But in an entirely different way."

There was hidden meaning in his words, and even he was still trying to translate for himself. Being around this woman, and the feelings she was wrestling up, was as terrifying as it was exhilarating.

Before Anna had a chance to respond, Lorenzo interrupted them. "I hope you two enjoyed your meal." Nick reluctantly drew his gaze from Anna, wishing for another moment alone. "My granddaughter mentioned overhearing your conversation earlier about whether the place would suit your needs for the dinner. Gina thought that maybe you would be interested in taking a look at one more spot." The old man hesitated. "It's different than what people are usually looking for, so it's not something we usually show. But if you'd like, I could…"

"We'd love to see it," Anna said, looking at the old man with a glimmer of hope.

They followed him across the patio and toward a different entrance to the main building than they'd originally come from. The old and weathered antique door was wide enough to allow three people through the entrance, and if Nick were to guess, it was probably once used for storage.

The cool, faintly musty air met them first as Lorenzo propped open the door. An old stone floor gave way a few feet in to a set of shallow steps that Lorenzo led them down. Images of Dracula's castle and serial killer torture chambers entered his head for a second, and he almost laughed as he caught Anna's eye, wondering if she felt the same way.

"Before this place was a restaurant, my father made an attempt at wine making," Lorenzo explained, his voice echoing back to them. "For thirty years, our family labored to fulfill this passion, but it was tough work, and by the time I was ready to take the helm, I had my own passion. Opening this restaurant. However, the old wine cellar remains."

They reached the bottom of the stairs and Lorenzo turned on another light and the large, almost cavernous basement lit up.

The place felt timeless. Authentic. Unique.

Against the back and side walls were abandoned wine caskets, large wooden barrels stacked against each other, three barrels high. The floor in front of the barrels was cleared out except for about five round wooden tables with benches and antique chairs gathered around for seating. Without the natural light from the large windows upstairs, the room was darker but still warm and inviting thanks to the light from the small sconces hanging from the ceiling. The setting was intimate and some would even say...romantic.

Anna exhaled as she looked around, shivering slightly. "This place is lovely." Her eyes were brighter now with excitement. "It's perfect." She looked back at him. "What do you think?"

He couldn't help but grin at her enthusiasm. "It's almost...magical."

Something passed in her eyes as he said this, some intimacy between them that had his throat constricting as he tried to force the breath into his lungs.

It seemed that a lot of things that he once might have

written off had more hidden appeal than he'd ever thought possible.

~

ANNA CROSSED her arms behind her back as she and Nick strolled down a row of grapevines, killing time until Lorenzo could finish drawing up the paperwork. Even though the restaurant was no longer in the wine-making business, according to Lorenzo, they still harvested their grapes to be sold to a local winery.

She looked up at the sky just as a breeze came up, sweeping her hair back and off her neck, surprised to see fast-incoming clouds, dark spots against the once bright sunny sky.

"Do you want to head back?" Nick asked, following her gaze up.

She looked around at the beauty of the valley around them. Here, she could forget about what waited for them back at the estate, could escape her past and just breathe again. She wanted to prolong this moment, not end it. "Not just yet."

He nodded quietly. It had been like this ever since that moment on the patio. The energy growing between them was tangible, and if she held up her finger, she was sure she would feel a pulse.

Another gust of wind tossed her hair, this time across her face, and she worked to pin it back just as an earth-shattering crack sounded above them, making her jump. A heavy drop of rain hit the top of her head, followed by another on her shoulder. Then a torrent of water unleashed down on them, and she felt her hand being caught up in Nick's as he led her racing to a large apple tree.

She laughed and glanced down to see that, in the space of those seconds, her clothes had become drenched and now clung to her body. She met Nick's gaze, expecting to see a hint of a smile at their predicament, but his face was serious, his eyes dark and intense as he studied her.

Then she knew.

She knew that in about two seconds he was going to kiss her.

Her gaze dropped to his lips. Lips that she longed to feel on hers.

He took a step forward, his hand coming up to push a swath of hair from her glistening face. Impatiently, she waited to feel the shock of his lips against hers, but it was like he was taking his sweet time as his hand went around her waist, pulling her against him, and he searched her face, his own so serious. Finally, he dipped his head down, and she held her breath until she felt his lips, his mouth hot and hypnotic as it moved against hers almost like a dance. A slow, sensual dance that didn't take her any time to learn the rhythm.

Anna felt like she was falling back into a void as the emotions and long-repressed desires overcame her, but she found the sturdy trunk of the apple tree holding her up. Holding them both up. She could melt against it as Nick's body molded against hers.

It was like she'd lived this moment before.

Like she knew the contours of his face that she held now in her hands, the familiar strength in his arms, his fingers as they tightened against her. It was new and wonderful but also almost like coming...

Home.

Had he always been there? Somewhere in her subconscious, a possibility never realized? Had she hidden her true feelings for him all this time as a protection against the pain of his inevitable rejection?

Because right now, everything about this moment felt right.

Her heart was beating so hard that she wondered if he could feel it. His lips were leaving a trail down her neck, kissing every bit of exposed skin, and she wanted to hold on to this moment always.

"*Signorina*?" Lorenzo.

Nick appeared to have heard him, too, as he took a step back. But his gaze will still on her, and there was a promise in those eyes that left her shivering.

Lorenzo called again, and she bit her lip to stop from laughing. A strange hysteria took over her suddenly tingling body as her mind whirled from the range of emotions she'd experienced in the space of a minute. She was losing her mind.

"I think Lorenzo is worried about your virtue," Nick said, his mouth widening into a sultry smile.

"Was I in danger of it being compromised?" she asked breathlessly.

"Absolutely." Nick looked down, taking her hand in his. "Guess it's time we return to the party. If we hurry, you'll be just in time for the bachelorette party."

She groaned and leaned into him for one last moment. But she didn't care, not really. The thought of such a silly, frivolous event might have horrified her before, but now she needed space from Nick St. Claire.

Because she didn't think, if given the option, she'd have minded being compromised.

Just a little.

CHAPTER 11

THE BAR where they were meeting for tonight's bachelor party was dark, seedy, and loud—and pretty much everything you'd want for such an event. Over at one of several pool tables, their crew of five were already imbibing their third round of shots and pretending not to notice the covetous glances several women were throwing their way.

Boisterous and halfway to drunk, the guys were having a great time, even if the usual salacious entertainment common to these events wasn't part of the itinerary. Knowing their limited options in Napa—and wanting to make sure the groom wasn't suffering from a serious hangover in time to say his vows—Dax had already had his wild bachelor weekend in Vegas last month. Tonight was meant to be a final low-key heyday before he was officially a married man.

Nick raised his hand to the bartender and ordered a gin and tonic. Unlike the rest of the guys, he was forgoing the shots and keeping his drinks down to two for the night. Keeping his senses about him was a far better idea than having too good of a time, particularly since the more his guard was down, the more likely he might do something really stupid later on.

Like try to resume what he and a certain beautiful blonde had started today in that vineyard. He still couldn't believe what had happened, how damn good it was, and how much he wanted more.

He'd known Anna was dangerous, but the reasons were more complicated than he'd first thought. Sure, she was a reporter and could cause a whole crap load of problems if she got it in her head to use his career and her insider knowledge to give herself a leg up. But for some reason, that wasn't what he was worried about. She'd given him her word and somehow that was enough.

No, his concern was more about how he would ever stop wanting her. He had no doubt that having Anna in his life would be as addictive as any drug. Hell, she already was, especially as he thought about how pliant her mouth had been beneath his before becoming as fierce and demanding as his. Then there'd been her intoxicating scent, a scent that had stayed with him long after they'd ended their kiss.

The need and possessiveness that overcame him shook him to the core; it didn't align with his carefully laid out ideals of his future wife. These emotions were dangerous, out-of-control feelings that led to trouble.

Nick had barely been able to speak two words as they drove the ten minutes back to the house. But words hadn't been necessary as they sat in the car, the silence and tension thick between them, broken only by the rain still pounding the windshield. It had been good that he had tonight to get away from her presence and to get his thoughts together.

"Hey, Nick."

He looked up, noticing Dax was standing next to him, trying to get his attention for who knew how long. Dax shook his head. "Man, you're really out of it tonight. Any particular reason...or person?"

Nick ignored him and took a drink.

"Don't worry. Your secret is safe with me." Dax signaled for a drink, then rapped his knuckles against the top of the bar as he waited, a far-off look in his eyes.

"Janie's going to love the place we found," Nick offered in assurance, wondering if that was the reason for Dax's sudden nervous energy.

"Yeah. That's great."

Nick studied his brother. "Hey, is everything all right?"

Dax forced a smile, his lips tight. "Yeah. Everything is great."

"You're going to have to do better than that."

"It's nothing. Only...have you ever made a bad choice in the past that you wanted to forget?"

"Too many to count."

"Yeah. But what if one of those choices, you...you couldn't get away from? And you wonder now if you should have handled things differently. Been more up-front from the start so it wasn't hanging over you months and years down the line."

Nick had an inkling that he knew what Dax was talking about. If he was right, then it wasn't his place to bring it up now. It was on Dax. "You're going to need to be more specific here. Is this something that has to do with Janie? With the wedding?"

There was a shout of victory, and Nick looked over at the pool table, where the game had ended, Jake and Chris congratulating themselves as the winners. Dax blinked a few times, as if clearing his head and realizing where he was, before giving his head a shake. He laughed and Nick could tell that whatever moment they were going to have had passed. "Nah, never mind. I'm just overthinking things. Must be the pressure of the wedding. You going to come join us?" he asked as the bartender delivered him his drink.

"On my way," Nick said and grabbed his own.

"How do you think the girls are holding up?" Dax asked as they walked.

Nick smiled, remembering his suggestion to Janie about tonight's entertainment. "We could probably see for ourselves if we wanted."

"You don't think that would be too presumptuous? Me crashing her bachelorette party?"

Possibly. But since all Nick wanted was to see Anna being forced to sing some cheesy country song in a horrible if not endearing off-key voice, he wasn't sure he was the best guy to ask. Instead, he said, "She'll think you missed her."

Sure, Nick had just been congratulating himself on getting some time away from the woman to clear his head, but this was one act he couldn't miss.

"Here we are," Janie said, stopping on the sidewalk in front of a set of bright red doors. The "future bride" rhinestoned tiara that she'd been crowned with earlier that night sat a little askew on her head as she grinned back at her bridal party, a glimmer of mischief in her eyes.

Oh, Lord. "You're not taking us to a strip bar, are you?" Anna asked in horror as images of Chippendale wannabes thrusting about in black bikinis flooded her mind.

Megan laughed. "You're safe. We did that weeks ago."

"Don't worry, you'll see soon enough," Janie added mysteriously and opened the door.

Unlike the brightly lit, upscale pub where they'd eaten

dinner, this place had a more local, down-to-earth vibe with its high blue ceilings, vintage photos that covered every wall, and sparse lighting. It wasn't particularly crowded, which wasn't unusual for a Thursday night. Anna took it as a good sign that there weren't any errant poles or bikini-clad strippers.

After showing their IDs and confirming who they were to the guy at the door—as if their outfits of matching black tank tops that declared them part of the "bride squad" could leave any doubt—they were led to a table in the back.

Maybe the place wouldn't be as bad as she thought, considering that, without the pub's bright overhead lighting, she could finally sink into the background, using the time to think about what happened today. Something she had barely had a chance to reflect on since walking back into the Van Hollinses' and being rushed upstairs with the other girls to get ready for the night. But the mood had been high and energetic and, combined with the swell of emotions still resonating through her from that kiss, catching. So she'd laughed and let herself enjoy the moment, the primping and hair fluffing, the flattery that filled the room before they'd filed onto the bus for more frivolity as they headed to dinner.

Now that she could finally catch her breath, Anna was ready to dissect every moment of her time with Nick. Every touch. Every smell. Every emotion that had flooded her as he held her tightly to him. Especially the one that evoked a memory, a dream if you will, of something that she'd never consciously remembered. Of kissing or wanting to kiss Nick St. Claire.

It was a crazy thought. She'd hated Nick back in high school. He was incredibly hot, brilliant, and ambitious, and the object of nearly every girl's fantasy. Every girl but this girl. It was a source of pride to her. Or so she'd thought.

Had she pretended she was immune to Nick's charms when really she'd been like every other girl in that school who had been drawn to that unexplainable something about Nick St. Claire had? Heck, could she be falling for the guy now, after all this time?

"Here you go." It was their waitress, who came bearing a tray of shots that Janie had ordered first thing on arriving.

Anna grabbed one and threw it back, hoping the fire of the liquor might burn away every thought and memory that was now fresh and present in her conscious.

Nope. Still there.

The guy who'd escorted them to their table returned to speak quietly to Janie, who clapped excitedly at whatever he said. "Okay. Everything's set," Janie announced. "I want you all to know right now that participation is not optional."

Why was she looking at Anna when she said this?

"Do you guys remember, back at Chi Omega, when we'd hold our own *American Idol* competitions? We had those little trophies made up and the winner would get to be queen for the week? Well, in the spirit of that, I thought, what would be better than to relive some of those great moments? We're doing karaoke!"

Karaoke? Could it be a coincidence that Nick had joked about this very thing when they negotiated their deal?

"It's already been arranged with the manager, thanks to Nick, our best man, who we'll all need to give a big thanks to the next time we see him."

Oh, Anna would be happy to tell him how thankful she was when she—

"Don't look so alarmed," Megan said from next to her,

smiling. "We all suck, so it will be assured mutual humiliation."

"Hey, speak for yourself," Trish said, pretending outrage. "I do a mean Dolly Parton. Just watch."

"What a great idea," Sara said in a tone that suggested the opposite, just before waving the server over to place another order of drinks. "So, who's going to go first?"

"It's only fair that we give Anna some idea of the competition she's going to be up against, which was why I thought that Trish, Megan, and I could get up and do that number, remember—"

"Oh, my God. I almost forgot!" Trish chimed in. "The Abba one."

"Fun." Sara was the only one who looked less excited than Anna, something the other women picked up on.

"Oh, come on, Sara," Trish said and nudged her shoulder. "You could have been in Chi-O if you'd wanted, but you went with Pi Beta Phi instead. It's not our fault you missed all the fun."

"But never fear," Janie added, coming to her feet. "You'll definitely get your chance. I think there's a Spice Girls number with our name on it. And Anna?" The mischievous grin Janie gave her told her she was in trouble. "I've got your number already lined up, too."

"Actually"—Anna cleared her throat, keeping her voice low and husky—"I might be coming down with something, so it's probably not a good idea—"

"Sorry. I'm not taking no for an answer. You have the next couple of songs to rest your throat and then you and me? We're on."

Good grief. Singing. In public.

In her book, it was right up there with stripping naked and gyrating on a pole, which, come to think of it, Nick had made a similar reference to—at least about being naked and singing. (The pole theme was entirely hers.)

The server had just arrived with their next order of drinks when the three sorority sisters took their positions in the front of their small audience and burst into song, their hands wildly waving around like bad spirit fingers. Anna grabbed one of the drinks and threw it back. She was certainly going to need it.

Only thirty minutes later, having been inducted into the karaoke family with hers and Janie's duet to "You Don't Own me," then a rousing chorus of "We are Family," where all the women joined in, followed by Trish, Megan, and Sara's rendition of the Dixie Chicks' "Goodbye Earl," Anna was finding that the horror of getting up in front of a room full of strangers to sing her heart out wasn't nearly as daunting as she had once thought.

All right. She could admit that it was kind of fun.

She had even decided to surprise Janie with this next song, a solo that she was going to nail and would earn her the crown of Karaoke Queen for the night—along with the prize of a pair of Tiffany silver hoop earrings. In the meantime, maybe she'd better lay off the endless rounds of shots they'd all been drinking.

Anna again took her position in front of the growing crowd. "This next song I'd like to dedicate to my beautiful, sweet sister, Janie, who, although I might not have grown up knowing and loving, is fast becoming one of my best friends."

Sheesh, she was being unusually sappy, but she couldn't say she regretted it. The joy it evidently brought Janie, who wiped away what looked suspiciously like a tear before she blew her several air kisses, was worth it. Heck, maybe Anna had even meant some of it.

The beginning notes of the next song started, and she clutched the microphone, hoping she could carry a few of those challenging notes that she had so ambitiously thought she could when she selected it. Taking a breath, she belted out the opening words to her favorite song from Dylan Charles.

She smiled a little at the approving shouts from the girls when her voice actually cooperated and sang out the words loud and clear. After warming up to the song, she grinned, loving the words and how they evoked memories of a certain rain-soaked kiss under an apple tree, and of feeling an excitement and acceptance that she couldn't remember feeling in a long time, if ever.

It was then that her gaze locked in on another person in the audience she hadn't noticed before. A guy with dark, wavy hair, a cocky but breathtaking grin, and eyes that burned back at her with a familiar intimacy.

Her stomach did a healthy somersault, and she nearly lost her breath for the next line as she recognized him.

Nick. The teenage fantasy she'd never known she'd wanted.

Nick, Dax, and the other groomsmen had arrived almost ten minutes before Anna took the spotlight. They set themselves as far back from the other patrons as they could, enjoying the show but wanting to remain invisible for as long as possible.

To say the night had become infinitely more entertaining the moment they caught the women's surprisingly energetic performances was an understatement. Dax had even managed to get some footage on his cell phone. For posterity's sake, of course.

When Anna had sashayed up there, giving a surprisingly moving dedication to her sister before ripping out a number that showed off her low, sultry vocal skills he hadn't known she was capable of, he—like every other warm-blooded man in this crowd—was entranced.

She likely had no idea how incredibly sexy she was standing up there, all eyes drawn to her. Her honey-blonde hair caught the light, her eyes shone with mischief, and those velvety-soft lips were red and luscious and crying to be kissed again. She was mesmerizing, and he was fast realizing that he was in serious trouble.

All Nick could think about doing was taking this woman somewhere private and quiet and showing her just how special and wonderful and infinitely beautiful and desirable she was.

When she met his gaze, he almost completely lost his composure. In that moment, it was as if everyone around them disappeared, and she was performing for him alone.

She smiled knowingly and unlocked her gaze from his, and he could breathe again. He glanced around at the other guys, wondering if they had noticed his reaction, but they were all nodding and smiling at Anna as she continued to sing.

No wiser to the fact that Nick's whole life seemed to just shift. Everything he'd wanted and wished for himself changing so quickly and suddenly in the space of a moment.

The song came to an end, and instead of passing off the microphone to the next person, she held it. "It's come to my attention that we have a few party crashers at our little sing-off tonight. Gentlemen?" she said and pointed to their table, all heads whipping back to see the crashers. "I think it's only fair that you subject yourself to the same humiliation as us ladies and get your butts up here for the next song. Come on," she said, moving to the karaoke machine to type something in.

"What do you say, guys?" Dax asked. "Should we show the ladies our boy band skills?" Dax asked.

"Hell yeah," seemed to be the consensus.

On the way up, Janie grabbed Dax, and instead of appearing miffed at their spying, she planted a kiss on him. Dazed, Dax followed the guys and took the mike from Anna as everyone laughed.

Nick glanced over Dax's shoulder at the screen, where the song they were going to sing was listed.

"I Feel Pretty" from *West Side Story*.

Funny.

Dax didn't look shaken, though. "Challenge accepted. Ladies, prepare to be impressed."

CHAPTER 12

NICK FLIPPED over to his back, trying to find the sleep that he needed if he was going to be a human tomorrow. Make that today, since technically, the clock was ticking past two a.m.

He closed his eyes, desperate for the welcome bliss of sleep, but instead, he saw the stunned look on Anna's face when he'd kissed her under that tree. Felt her body's response to his embrace, tightening and pulling him closer, her fingers on the back of his neck, wrapped in the ends of his hair, and his body's instant reaction to the sensation.

Good God. He threw off the blanket and sat up. This wouldn't do. He had to do something else, something active and physical to get his mind off that woman.

Twenty minutes later, he was gliding in the cool, silky water of the Van Hollinses' pool, swimming his ninth lap. Here, under the stars and the faint light of the moon, he was able to push away the lingering thoughts and memories and focus on the sound of the water around him as he glided through until he reached the end and turned around and did it again.

His breathing was measured and methodical, his libido and self-control firmly in check.

He reached the end of the pool, about to go under to flip around when he saw a pair of bare feet waiting on the edge. He looked up, blinking the water away in case it was an apparition.

Nope. It was Anna.

How long had she been there? Had his thoughts summoned her in the flesh or was this a mirage, a by-product of fatigue and fantasy?

"You could try to keep it down out here. Some people are trying to sleep," she said before sitting down to dangle her feet in the pool.

Yep. Definitely real.

He wiped his hair back from his face and lifted himself from the pool to sit next to her, his breath loud from the exertion.

"Funny, but you seem to be the only person affected. Are you sure you weren't spying on me?" he asked, staring at her long, bare legs, appreciating the sight of the smooth skin, the shapely calves, and the delicate arch of her foot.

"Of course not!"

Her denial stood in stark contrast to the guilty flush on her face, the biting of her bottom lip. It gave him a satisfying thrill to know that maybe he wasn't alone tonight in his rest-lessness. However, he declined to push further, instead reaching for the towel behind her and using it to wipe the excess water from his chest and arms.

He risked another glance at her. Anna's eyes were wide and curious as she watched the towel's movement over his body, her lips parting—

"Actually," she said, her voice an octave higher than

usual, "I was thinking about how we never got the fifteen minutes you promised me as part of our deal. I've more than held up my end of the bargain today."

"If memory serves, wasn't the deal supposed to include *naked* karaoke?"

"Does it count that I *felt* naked, standing up there in front of everyone? I don't know if I've ever felt so vulnerable, and that's counting the first time one of my stories was published."

He could relate. There was something unnerving about putting yourself out there for the public's unfettered examination and opinion. It got easier, with time, but he was well aware that he cared a great deal about public opinion, probably more than he should. "Well, what would you like to know?"

From the pocket of her gray hoodie, she took out her phone, turning on the recording device and setting it down on a dry spot. "For starters, if you win the senate race, what are some of the issues that you're interested in pursuing? What will your platform be?"

She certainly got down to business. No soft pitches to start the interview. Fortunately, he didn't have to think about it. He easily listed a handful of causes that he wanted to bring to his fellow senators' attention, including water reclamation, sustainable energy, and making higher-education grants and opportunities more available for low- to middle-income families.

Unlike when he'd ever brought these interests up to Sara —or Madison or Jennifer before her—Anna's eyes didn't glaze over. In fact, she pushed him on the issues and came up with questions that he hadn't seen coming. She really was interested and he couldn't explain how good it was to know this.

When the fifteen minutes turned into twenty, he didn't care. Their debate was scintillating enough he'd have carried on another hour, but the yawn that Anna gave made him realize how late it was and that, as much as he'd like to spend the entire night talking with her, they both needed to get some rest.

"You're exhausted. We should probably head in."

She nodded. "You're right, especially since we're supposed to be up in"—she turned off the voice recorder and looked at her phone for the time—"four hours if we're going to make the bus for the hot air balloon excursion."

"You're still planning on going?" He had thought she would have passed, after the night's events.

"It's one of the few things I'm looking forward to," she confessed.

"I can't say I'm of the same mind." When she glanced at him curiously, he expanded, "I have a bit of a hang-up when it comes to...heights."

She laughed. "You're kidding."

"I wish I was. Been afraid ever since my dad first took me and Dax skiing up in Big Bear when I was ten years old. I screamed my head off until the lift reached solid ground again. It was not a pretty sight—or sound."

She held her stomach as she laughed. "Poor you. What I wouldn't give to have seen that. I bet that put a damper on your big ski trip. Was your dad disappointed?"

His dad's embarrassment and then anger when Nick surprised him—and the woman he was with—when he'd arrived earlier than usual back in their suite was forever etched in his mind. "In more ways than one," he said before he could stop himself.

"You couldn't have been the first kid to have that reaction."

He sighed and leaned back as he tried to decide whether he was ready to share this with Anna, when up to this moment, he'd never told anyone. Not Dax and especially not his mother. But something about this woman made him feel like he wanted to help her understand more about him. "It wasn't so much that I chickened out on finishing my lesson with the instructor he'd hired as it was that I walked in on him in a...somewhat compromising position with one of the young interns from his office."

"No," she said, raising her hand to cover her mouth.

"I think that was Dad's sentiment, too. It was the day that the image I had of him as this great, admirable man cracked a little." As was the belief he'd held that family, their life, was perfect. He saw a lot of things differently after that day.

She placed her hand over his. "I'm sorry, Nick. That's rough. Did...did you ever talk to your dad about this? Or talk with anyone? I mean, that's a lot for a ten-year-old kid to process."

He shook his head. "Didn't see any point. Dax was barely six at the time, and he wouldn't have understood things. And my mother...well, I started to once, but I swear she knew what I was going to say and headed me off before I could get the words out. After that, however, I noticed things more, like how frequently he would stay late at work or would go away on weekends for work."

"Do you think your mother knew about his affairs?"

"I'm pretty sure she did, but it's not something that we ever discussed. Frankly, the whole thing was depressing." Nick tilted his head up toward the sky, staring at the sea of stars that twinkled back at them. "Look at that. You never see that in the city. You know," he said when she remained silent, her attention now on the sky above them, "we talked about this earlier. About whether I want my marriage to be like my parents'. And I want to clarify. There were good things about their marriage. They were usually united when it came to raising Dax and me, and there was no end to the family vacations and family dinners we had that I still have fond memories of. But I like to think that when I finally commit myself in marriage to someone, mutual respect, trust, *and fidelity* will be part of the package."

"At the very least."

He glanced over to find her smiling softly at him. He couldn't stop looking at her. At those wide blue-gray eyes that reminded him of the sea on a stormy day, fathomless and mysterious but also beautiful. At the subtle curve of her jaw. At the soft plushness of those lips that he'd tasted once and he knew he needed to taste again.

Before he could second-guess his decision, Nick leaned over and kissed her lips more softly this time, careful to keep his hands grounded firmly under him. Instantly, her eyes fluttered shut, something she'd done the last time he'd kissed her, and he wondered what she was thinking or if she was capable of thought—much like him.

But unlike before, when the fierceness of the rain had brought out an equally fierce and intense reaction in him, this time he began slowly, leisurely, as he savored the sensation of her lips, the touch of his tongue to hers, tentative at first before she opened her mouth and welcomed him in. He wanted to wrap his hands in her hair and hold her face against his, but he made himself go slow, his hands remaining at his sides.

Anna held no similar compunction as she raised her hand to his chest. The area where she touched—as well as a few other areas that were making it impossible to think straight—flared hot and alive. Nick's need for this woman, the sensations she brought him, was almost overpowering.

Despite his promise to keep it easy and simple, his hand lifted to hold on to her waist before gliding farther down to the curve of her hip and along the back of her upper thigh. She shivered against the light touch but didn't pull away, if anything tightening her leg against his.

She was going to kill him.

He would give anything to lay her out under the moonlight, to strip that sweatshirt off and let his gaze roam her body, followed by his hands, his mouth...but something reined him in. Told him that he didn't want to rush this. With Anna, he needed to take his time.

Reluctantly, he pulled his lips from hers, exhaling a sigh of near frustration. Her eyes opened slowly, the desire in their cloudy depths bringing a sharp tug of need low in his gut. It reaffirmed his decision to slow things down.

She seemed to be of the same opinion as she suddenly realized her position and, pulling her leg away, scrambled to her feet. "That was..." She raised her gaze to his again, appearing nervous. Uncertain.

He smiled. "Amazing. And something we're going to explore another time, I assure you."

"I was going to go with something more like...impetuous. And best not to ever happen again."

Yeah. Sure she was. But he could let her have that and as much time as she needed to come to grips with the fact that something was happening between them. Something she wasn't going to be able to run from.

"Whatever you say."

She leaned down and grabbed her phone and returned it to her pocket. "I had better try and catch some sleep. Six a.m. is coming alarmingly soon."

He nodded, unable to keep the smile from his face. "Sweet dreams."

She walked away, her arms wrapped around her as if warding off a sudden chill.

And his heart, for the first time in a long time, felt light.

Hopeful.

~

ANNA ARRIVED downstairs a full fifteen minutes before the designated time, which was a first for her. She knew that, with as little sleep as she'd had the past few days, caffeine— and a lot of it—would be her best friend.

She was almost to the kitchen when the sound of raised voices reached her, angry whispers that sounded like Dax and...Sara? She slowed, curiosity overriding courtesy as she strained to hear what they were talking about.

"I owe Janie the truth," Dax was saying. "Let her make the decision whether it was insignificant or not."

"Don't be an idiot," Sara said in a sharp tone that Anna had never heard before. "There's no reason she has to know at all. I'm not going to tell her, if that's what you're worried about. And if you cared for her as you say you do, then you wouldn't want to hurt her by telling her about something that has been over for years, especially when you two are supposed to be getting married tomorrow."

"I let you talk me out of telling Janie about us two years ago because I believed that you were right and whatever you and I did in those early weeks when we all met up in Mexico had no bearing on my new relationship with Janie. I thought telling her would ruin any chance I had of making a go with her. I let you talk me out of it again when you and Nick started dating each other, reminding me that you and I made a mistake and there was no use bringing up the skeletons from the closet when it would only hurt those we loved. But now—" His voice cracked, and he took a minute to continue. "I don't think that Janie and I can build a solid foundation together, a new life as husband and wife, when our foundation is built on a lie."

"Don't be ridiculous, Dax," Sara said, this time laughing at him. "You never lied to her about anything. I never told her about our summer camp romance, and I never told her we were hooking up those late Mexican nights after she'd been strolling arm-in-arm with you on the beach moments before. You never were put in the situation where you had to lie. Don't be so melodramatic."

"An omission on something as important as this is the same as a lie."

There was the sound of a hand slamming down on the counter. "Damnit, Dax. You're going to ruin everything. Have you thought about who is going to get hurt the most here? Janie. She will be losing her faith in not only you but also me, her best friend. And once Nick hears about this, he's bound to be hurt, too. To hear that you—his own brother—deceived him about screwing his ex-girlfriend."

Anna was shocked. Who knew that the quiet, supportive Sara had been hiding this secret from everyone, most of all her purported friend?

"Come on, Sara. Let's be honest here. The only person you're really concerned about in all of this is yourself. You're worried you're going to lose your best friend, sure, but most of all you're worried that whatever chance you had of reigniting something with Nick, of getting into his good graces again and being welcomed back into the St. Claire circle of influence, will go up in smoke."

"Janie will never forgive you, Dax. If you do this, if you

tell her that you were professing your early love to her while slipping away to see me and that you've been keeping this from her for two years, she's going to dump you and any future you were hoping to have with her."

"Maybe. But she has the right to know everything about me, the good and the bad, before she commits herself to me. I'm sorry that this is going to hurt the people I care the most about, but the sooner you resign yourself to this happening the better, because nothing you can do or say is going to make me change my mind again."

There were footsteps on the stairs above her; someone was going to break up this little chat any minute—and see Anna standing not so innocently outside the door.

"Morning!" she sang as she walked into the kitchen, pretending she didn't see Dax turn away to collect himself or Sara's face furious and red. Anna bit back the impulse to confront the woman for the deception that she'd played against Janie and Nick. Dax hadn't been any better, though, even if he was finally coming to his senses. With cheerfulness she didn't feel, she smiled at them both.

"Morning, Anna," Dax said, his head dipped down in shame. Rightfully so. "You know, I'm going to take these mugs of coffee up to my fiancée and see if I can cajole her into sleeping in a little longer. Janie won't admit it but I know she's exhausted, and her excitement caused her to overestimate how much this wedding was going to take out of her. Would you mind explaining to everyone why we're not there?"

Was Dax going to have the heart-to-heart with Janie now? And if so, would there even be a spa day or rehearsal dinner or...wedding?

But all she said to Dax was, "Of course. Go, shoo."

She watched as Dax walked away, his shoulders

hunched over, before meeting Sara's gaze and asking, "How did you sleep?"

Sara looked at her uneasily, as if trying to decide whether Anna had heard any of the conversation. Anna kept her smile easy as she poured herself a cup of coffee and waited.

"Not very well, to tell you the truth. In fact, I think I might take a page out of the groom's book and stay in my room and veg until it's time for our spa appointments."

"Absolutely. Great idea," Anna said and followed Sara's progress out of the kitchen from the rim of her mug. She heard a brief greeting in the hall as the woman crossed paths with someone.

Not just anyone, if Anna wasn't mistaken. Nick.

Despite the conversation she'd just overheard and the heartache she felt for her sister, she couldn't help but grin shyly at Nick as he walked in.

The sun had barely popped up over the eastern ridge, bathing the kitchen—and his face—in its first light. He looked tired, his usually clean-shaven jawline sprinkled with stubble. His hair was still wet, as if he'd just climbed out of the shower before slipping on those soft, faded denim jeans and the long-sleeved bluish-green tee shirt. There was definite fatigue around the corners of his eyes, but his eyes were bright and alert, particularly as he caught a glimpse of her alone in the kitchen. His face broke into an uncharacteristically broad smile, and her heart did a strange tap dance inside her chest.

He didn't hesitate as he walked deliberately toward her, his eyes burning with the same need he'd shown last night, even as he'd sent her along to bed like a little girl. Without a word, he took the coffee mug from her hand and pulled her to him, cupping her head in the palm of his hand so he could better access her lips, his minty breath mixing with hers. And even though she'd cursed him last night for the mix of emotions he'd caused, now, back under the warm expertise of his mouth, her resolve to keep far away from his lips today quickly melted away and she was only too happy to wrap her arms around his shoulders. To push herself up on her tiptoes so she could access the back of his neck better as she tousled his hair in her fingers, blissful in this solitary moment.

Was this what it was like to have someone in your life you truly cared about? To look forward to their smiles, their touch, their kisses, even the bristly roughness of their unshaven jaw against your chin? If so, she could definitely get used to this.

The obnoxious sound of honking, coming from the front of the house, brought them apart.

"Looks like the bus is here," Nick said. He looked around the kitchen as if realizing for the first time that they were alone. "Where is everyone? Janie said six thirty sharp, and I swore I heard Dax earlier."

If he knew what was good for him, Dax was on his knees begging—no, groveling—for Janie's forgiveness, promising to make it up to her for the rest of their lives.

"Um, you did, but Dax said to go along without them. Something about letting Janie sleep in."

"Yeah, I just saw Sara and she was heading back to bed, too. Does that mean it's just going to be the two of us?"

He appeared entirely too hopeful as he smiled at her, and she laughed, resting her hand on his chest. She enjoyed the feeling of being able to touch him, of feeling his heart beat under her palm without needing to offer an explanation for the intimacy. "Unless you know how to operate a hot air balloon—and with your fear of heights I find that hard to believe—then I wouldn't exactly say we'll be alone."

"Let's get out of here before anyone else changes their mind. You brought along earplugs just in case?"

She grinned. "I figure I'll throw you over if the screaming gets to be too much."

CHAPTER 13

ONE MISSISSIPPI. *Two Mississippi. Three Mississippi.*

The sensation of floating had Nick's stomach ready to come up his throat, but he didn't dare risk opening his eyes just yet. His fingers gripped the side of the carriage in which he, Anna, Jake, Megan, and the balloon operator were suspended.

He became aware of Anna's arm on his, her hand around his waist.

"It's progress," she said. "You're not screaming."

"Give me time."

A gust hit his face, and he used the chance to take in deep breaths.

He was being ridiculous, he knew, but that didn't change the way his heart was beating a million miles a minute; his hands were drenched in sweat, his breath labored. A few more seconds passed. Maybe longer. Then the rising seemed to stop and they moved in a forward motion, which helped his stomach stop flipping.

"Are we still climbing?" he asked.

"Nope. I think we're at the height we're going to be at, and Nick...you've got to see this. It's so beautiful."

Her voice was filled with a calm wonder and he grew curious, slowly opening his eyes to the vista ahead. There were rows upon rows of grapevines, their lush green leaves and the rich reddish-brown soil visible from high above. The slopes of the Napa hills went as far as the eye could see. Yet his gaze found a beautiful woman, with her hair in two youthful braids, a baseball cap drawn low over her eyes as protection from the sun, and her mouth open slightly as she took in the view. The tight red tee shirt she'd worn for this morning's excursion was cut low in a vee, exposing her neck and the skin below it. He wanted to press a kiss there along the side, just below her jaw, but he couldn't because he was too afraid to move his legs in case they buckled.

Or worse, he lost his balance and fell forward into the abyss. He was doing okay, for now, as long as no one made any sudden movements.

They stayed quiet for a few minutes, enjoying the breeze that swirled around them and the calmness. With Megan and Jake snuggling together on the other end of the carriage and the operator focused on his job, it was like they really were up here alone.

"So, was it worth it?" Anna asked.

"I'll tell you if I live, but right now? Absolutely."

Anna moved her hand down his arm to rest on his hand. "It's too bad that everyone is missing this. It's my favorite thing by far."

"I'm certain most everyone is nursing serious hangovers. Janie particularly," he added, remembering how giddy she was on the shuttle back, going around kissing everyone and thanking them for being part of her and Dax's special day. "Hopefully they'll be okay in time for us to make our tee time this afternoon," he said, referencing the golf game Dax and the other groomsmen were scheduled to play while the women had a day of pampering at the spa.

"Yes. Maybe..." Anna looked away guiltily.

He studied her. "What? Did Dax mention something to you about canceling the game? Was he sick?" Her eye twitched, telling him that something was up and she was struggling with keeping it from him. "Hey. You can tell me. Did they have a fight?"

She nodded, turning to face him again, her eyes crinkled in the corners as she looked at him with concern. "It's just... just that I heard something earlier. In the kitchen. Between Dax and...Sara."

Oh, shit. That wasn't good.

"What exactly did you overhear?" he asked cautiously.

Anna glanced over her shoulder to where Megan and Jake were standing, still enthralled in their own conversation, not paying them any mind. "Remember, I'm just the messenger here, so don't throw me over if you don't like what I'm about to say." She took in a deep breath. "It seems that at some point before Dax and Janie were engaged—which I understand was also before you and Sara became an item—the two of them were...hooking up."

He worked to keep his frustration from his face. Not with Anna, but with Dax and Sara for being so careless with their conversation.

"Nick? Are you okay? Did you hear what I said?"

"Yeah. I heard you." He pinched the bridge between his nose, taking a moment.

"Crap. I knew I shouldn't have brought it up. You're angry."

He sighed. "I'm angry but not at you. I already knew about their affair, although not as soon as I would have liked. I discovered it after I started dating Sara, who Janie and Dax were hyping up as a great girl and my perfect match." He met her gaze. "It's the other part of why I ended things with her. It was too weird for me to be with someone who had slept with my baby brother. So you can rest assured, you're not breaking my heart by telling me."

"You knew." She looked relieved. "I didn't shatter any illusions you might have had about Sara or your brother. How did you find out?"

"Just like you. I overheard them talking shortly after the engagement was announced. Hell, I was pissed. Pissed at Sara for lying to me all that time, making me feel like a fool. Pissed at Dax for pulling that shit in the first place and then covering it up. For having the gall to let me get tangled up with the same woman when there had been such a complicated history between them."

"And you never confronted them about it?"

"No." He should have, but he'd kept hoping that one of them would do the right thing and come clean.

"Do you think that Janie will be able to forgive him? Or will she end things like you did with Sara?"

He paused at the genuine concern in her voice for her sister, something she probably didn't even realize. "I don't know. I hope she can forgive him and move on. If there's one thing I know, it's that Dax really is in love with her and he's undoubtedly torn up about his mistake or he wouldn't be considering bringing it up now. And like I told you before, I already had some concerns where Sara was concerned, wondering whether she was into me as much has the St. Claire name and the free publicity showered on her just for being my girlfriend. It wasn't like she'd be the first person in my life who used me for their own self-interest."

Anna smiled. "If it means anything to you, I'm finding I like you *despite* your name and reputation."

Instantly, all the grief and disappointment from the last ten years of dating the wrong women faded away. "You know, since there's a good possibility that the house is combusting from the chaos unfurled by Dax's admission, we should make the best of our time up here and talk about important things like"—he reached out to play with one of her long braids, the plaits soft against his fingertips —"whether you had any hot erotic dreams about me last night. I know for a fact you made an appearance in mine."

She rolled her eyes. "Men. One-track minds."

"We have many tracks, but I will admit there's that one track that is always playing—even if only as background music."

"And it's playing right now?"

"Oh, yeah," he said, grinning at the warm flush on her cheeks. "But let's not get ahead of ourselves. First things first, you need to get a little closer." He lifted his arm, waiting for her to accept his offer.

She hesitated for only a moment before stepping between his arms, her face forward so they could look out at the view. He wrapped his arms around her, his hands settling around her waist. She leaned her head against his shoulder, sighing.

He could get used to this. To having this woman in his arms.

ANNA DIDN'T THINK anything could ruin her day as she stepped out of the town car and took Nick's offered hand before they strolled into the Val Hollins estate later that afternoon. Not even the itching and tingling on her arms that told her she'd be suffering from a sunburn in time for tomorrow's photo op—despite having slathered on a fifty SPF from head to toe this morning.

The day had been nothing short of perfect. Their exhilarating hot air balloon ride had been followed by brunch at a homey cafe in town, where they gorged themselves on pastries, fruit, omelets, and specialty coffee drinks. Being nestled under Nick's arm, his fingers playing intermittently with the braids in her hair and the skin at the back of her neck, while laughing and telling stories with Megan and Jake, had all felt so...right.

So this was what it felt like to be in a relationship that didn't end with her tiptoeing out of a guy's apartment in the early morning's light.

"You're back!" Janie called with excitement as they walked into the house. She was sitting in the large front room of the house, and she wasn't alone.

Anna's excitement level went from a ten to a minus one in the space of a second at the sight of none other than Kathryn St. Claire staring at her, or rather at her and Nick's joined hands. Anna welcomed the excuse to let go when Janie pranced over and gave her a tight hug.

"I was wondering when you guys were going to get back," Janie asked. "Did you have fun?"

From the excitement and happiness still emanating from Janie, Anna took a guess that Dax hadn't broken the news yet.

"It was great. Thanks for planning it," Megan answered and glanced around the room. "Hi, Mrs. Van Hollins," she said to the woman seated next to Kathryn. "Um, Janie, if you don't mind, Jake and I are going to go upstairs and rest up until our appointment."

"Go. Of course," Janie said, shooing them from the room. "I think everyone else is chilling at the pool if you change your mind. I'm sorry I couldn't join you guys, but Dax insisted I remain in bed and rest. He's always looking out for me."

Anna couldn't look at Dax right now, still angry and disappointed about the pain he was going to be causing someone as sweet as Janie.

Megan and Jake waved, looking relieved to leave the room that was growing tenser by the minute due to the fact that Nick and his mother seemed to be having some sort of some face-off.

Nick didn't flinch under Kathryn's stare. If anything, his stance seemed almost challenging, while Kathryn's eyes were cold as she stared at her son, nearly as cold as when she finally pulled them away to rest on Anna. The disdain in their depths assured Anna that Kathryn remembered who she was, even now.

"Anna, let me introduce you to my mother," Janie said and dragged Anna over to the couch. "Mother, this is Anna."

"Nice to meet you, Mrs. Van Hollins," Anna said politely. With light blonde hair, smooth and stretched skin, and hazel eyes, Elise was lovely, but she also seemed to be a little out of it, as if she was still coming down from the affects of too much Percocet.

Elise leaned forward the slightest bit, holding her hand out to Anna in one of those barely there handshakes. "Nice to meet you, Anna."

"And this is Nick's mother, Kathryn St. Claire. Maybe you already know each other? Nick went to high school with Anna," she explained to her mother.

"We have met. Nice to see you again, Anna," Kathryn said, holding her hand out. It was firm and cold, like her eyes that seemed to be telling Anna to keep her hands off her son.

Some things never changed.

"Wonderful to see you, too," Anna lied.

"Good afternoon, Mrs. Van Hollins. Mother," Nick said as he moved closer. Kathryn and Nick shared the same dark brown hair and eyes, but Kathryn's porcelain-white skin was a contrast to Nick's tanned skin. "I didn't think you were going to arrive until this evening."

"Fortunately, my plans changed and I saw no reason I shouldn't join Elise on her flight into Napa." Even ten years older, the woman was as imposing as ever. "It had been months since we caught up and, with Janie's excitement about meeting her new half sister, I thought I'd join the party."

"Yes. Janie was just telling us about how amazing you've been, stepping up as her maid of honor like you have," Elise Van Hollins said, smiling vaguely at Anna. "I imagine it can't have been easy coming into this thing without knowing a soul."

"Oh, Anna and Nick actually go way back," Kathryn interjected. "Anna once was hell-bent on destroying everything that Nick had worked so hard for when he was running for student body president, spinning lies and intrigue in her coverage for the school paper."

If Janie had missed the tension in the room before, her open-mouthed reaction as she stared at Nick's mother said she was now clued in.

"That's all water under the bridge," Nick said firmly. "In fact, in getting to know Anna again these past few days, I've been able to see things from a different perspective. God knows I wasn't a saint back then. We both did things we're not proud of."

"Yes, and how are you doing now, Anna?" Kathryn asked, barely waiting for Nick to finish. "Didn't you have some lofty aspirations of being a writer for the *LA Times*? Or was it *The New York Times*? How did that work out for you?"

The way the woman asked this told Anna that she knew very well where Anna was writing. She could play nice, up to a point. "I'm with *The Daily Rundown*. It's an online news magazine based out of San Francisco."

"I'm familiar with it. Another one of those gossip rags, isn't it? Nothing worth my time, I'm afraid."

"Okay, ladies, I have your tea," Sara said and sashayed into the room carrying a tray with a tea pot, cups, and an array of desserts that she set down on the coffee table.

In a gauzy cream dress that looked designer and well out of Anna's price range, her dark hair smooth and shining to perfection, Sara DeWinters looked like she belonged with Kathryn St. Claire and Elise Van Hollins. Anna, on the other hand, in her denim cutoff shorts and two long braids, whose plaits had loosened so that hair was poking out everywhere, looked like she'd just returned from a hoe-down.

"Thank you, Sara," Kathryn said, reaching for a teacup. "I can't say how much it pleases me to see you here today, watching out for our Janie and making sure she has what she needs before the big day."

Subtle dig to Anna? Check.

"Oh, please, I don't need anyone fussing over me. Well, not very much," Janie added and laughed. "And I assure you that Anna has given me more than enough attention. I know I'm not supposed to know anything about this," she said, "but she and Nick spent the entire afternoon yesterday trying to hunt down an alternate location for tonight's rehearsal dinner after our original venue's flooding."

"How...thoughtful," Kathryn said, turning that evil gaze

back on Anna.

"It was nothing. In fact, I rather enjoyed myself. As did Nick." Unable to resist, Anna smiled at the woman, refusing to let her think she was the same scared adolescent girl anymore. "Now, you'll have to excuse me, but with our spa appointments just an hour away, I need to get a few things squared away up in my room. It was nice to meet you, Mrs. Van Hollins. And Mrs. St. Claire...always a pleasure."

"You know, I think that's a great idea," Nick said and turned to go with her. "I probably should—"

"Actually, Nick darling," his mother said, stopping him in his tracks, "there were a few things I wanted to chat about while I have you. Can we go somewhere?"

Nick looked like he wanted to argue as he studied his mother, who was smiling angelically at him, but quickly saw the futility. "By all means, but it's going to have to be short since I still need to change before we head out to the golf course."

Anna didn't stick around to hear anything more since it felt like the opportunity for escape was fast closing. At the top of the stairs, she took in a deep breath and exhaled before moving down the hall to her room. She'd known Nick's mother was going to be here, so she shouldn't be as shaken as she was. However, she had hoped that her memory of the woman had been colored by the vulnerability of her youth, or at the least that the woman might have mellowed with age.

Neither of which seemed to be the case. She was still a peach.

But Anna wouldn't let her cast a shadow over this day. This thing that was happening between her and Nick was real, it was special, and nothing that woman could say or do could change that.

CHAPTER 14

NICK OPENED the door of what had once been the late Malcolm Van Hollins's study, a room that probably hadn't changed since his death. The room had all the personality of an old-school man-cave with the usual dark wood paneling, shelves of bound books against the wall, a massive fireplace, and a billiards table in the corner.

His mother followed him in and shut the door, moving slowly around the room, as if memorizing the pictures on the mantel and the books stacked next to an old recliner.

"That was an interesting arrival." She picked up a book and scanned the back. "You and that girl, hand-in-hand, almost like you're together. Would you care to tell me what's been going on over the past couple of days that would lead you to believe that taking up with that...that tabloid reporter is a good idea? Do you know how much damage she can do to this family?"

Her voice was soft but there was a definite edge there.

"Anna is hardly a girl, and definitely not just some tabloid reporter," Nick said, careful to keep his own tone even and not let her know her words angered him. "I can understand where your concerns are coming from, but I assure you that Anna isn't here to destroy me, my career, or our family, but merely to offer support to a sister she is just getting to know."

Okay, so there had been a different motive when she first arrived—to dig up a story that would help save her job and get her editor off her back, but he'd offered her a solution to that dilemma and, in the process, gotten so much more. Not that his mother needed to know the dirty details.

"Fine. For whatever reason, she's here. But I still can't imagine why you were holding her hand, Nicholas."

"You really can't imagine? How about because I have genuine feelings for Anna, who, I believe, happens to return those feelings."

"You believe? That's a large leap to make when the stakes are so high."

"Isn't that what finding love is about? Taking those leaps?"

He smiled, because he was realizing how true it was. Trusting Anna was a leap of faith, but also a leap into the unknown where her feelings for him were concerned, considering his track record.

Kathryn's face paled whiter than usual, her mouth frozen open, making speech impossible for a luxurious ten seconds. "Are you out of your mind? Did you just say...love? You're not honestly telling me that you love this girl? You've spent maybe one day with her."

"I don't know exactly what my feelings are for *Anna*," he emphasized, "but I look forward to finding out. For whatever reason, fate brought her back in my life and I'm not going to let the opportunity to get to know her better go by. You might want to get used to the idea of her being a regular part of my life because I have every intention of continuing this relationship when we're back in the city."

Kathryn St. Claire turned around and, finding a cognac-colored leather chair, sank down into it, crossing one elegant leg over the other. "And what do you think having this woman in your life is going to do for your career? She's a nobody. Whether or not Malcolm Van Hollins was her father, he never claimed her during his life and never let anyone know she was his. Who is her mother? I seem to remember the woman as some bohemian free spirit who spent more time traipsing the Amazonian jungle than raising her daughter. This woman you're so infatuated with has no connections, no social mores—not to mention no desire to learn them—and no career, at least not one worth mentioning. Writing for a silly gossip rag is hardly a career one would want for a wife—especially someone with your ambitions. And whether you like it or not, these things matter to people."

Nick ground his teeth at his mother's snobbery and her continued hatred for a woman she barely knew. "I couldn't care less whether she has the necessary connections or the pedigree you're so desperate for. Anna is the most genuine person I know—which is all that matters to me."

"You might not be saying that a few years from now when you're widening your net of voters for something more notable than a small state senate seat, such as a run for US Senate, or—should we be so lucky—something even bigger. You're going to need the votes and support from those conservative ranchers up north—ranchers like Sara DeWinters's family who've been a part of that landscape of politics for generations. Think of the power that you could harness by building an alliance with them. Think about the future generations you and Sara could build together, a legacy that would make the Kennedy clan look like the Clampetts."

He smiled at her desperate reference. "Well, I'm sorry to have to disappoint you, but there won't be an alliance with our family and the DeWinterses, not where I'm concerned. Unless you've forgotten, I tried things with Sara once only to discover we weren't meant to be."

"That's a load of crap. If there are any two people meant to be, it's you and Sara. You both have similar backgrounds, interests, ambitions—what more could you want in a partner?" She looked at him for a long moment before snorting. "As for love, I've been around a lot longer than you, dear boy, and I can safely say that there's no such thing, at least not in the romanticized way you're meaning. Not for people like you, like me."

"So the happy, loving couple outside these doors—Dax and Janie—they're not really in love? What, is that some kind of delusion they're both under?"

"You misunderstand me. I said for people like you. For Dax? He's always been a sweet and easygoing boy with no expectations and a desire to please everyone. Of course he'll be happy with Janie and they'll probably have a happy, easy life together. But you aren't your brother. You want more for yourself. What you need is a strong partner who can help you reach your goals."

"Like you and Dad, you mean."

His mother leaned back, not blinking as she met his gaze. "Yes, like your father and me. We both came into the marriage from a place of mutual respect. I saw an enigmatic man who could make people listen. He could inspire people and lead them. He saw in me not just someone who would take care of him and help push him for bigger things but also someone with the right connections and know-how to make things happen."

"Not to mention someone to look the other way when the indiscretions mounted up and the lies became harder to cover up."

She exhaled in exasperation. "Don't be naive, Nicholas. Those women never meant anything to your father. Not like I did. I understood that as much as him."

But Nick hadn't understood that. Not then and not now.

He turned away to look out the window. He shouldn't be surprised by his mother's candidness. He'd summarized their relationship himself in a similar fashion. His mother might have been perfectly fine knowing her husband was finding late-night solace in the arms of whatever young intern struck his fancy, but Nick didn't want the same thing for himself, and he sure as hell didn't want his wife—whoever that might be—being content with that picture either.

"All that is fine and good for you and Dad, but it's not enough for me, which is why the Sara DeWinterses of the world will never appeal to me," he said, turning to meet his mother's eyes. "I'm looking for something more. Someone who not only complements me as a partner but who"—he paused, remembering Anna's words—"who makes me laugh. Who is fun and exciting and challenges me every day and makes me look forward to the next one, when I get to wake up and do it all over again."

"You're being shortsighted. And stupid."

Nick didn't take offense at her words, however. Although they were harsh, he knew that his mother only resorted to such tactics when she ran out of arguments. As annoying and frustrating and pushy as his mother was, she said all this because she cared. Even though she disapproved of his choice, in the end she would support him, albeit reluctantly, just as she always did.

"I've done a decent job of following my own path these many years based on instinct, and that's what I'm going on now. Instinct," he said cheerfully. "If there isn't anything more, I really do need to change. I'll see you this evening." He stopped at the door. "And I expect you to be civil to Anna."

Kathryn didn't say anything more, but he felt her disapproval as he left the room. Something she'd have to get over because he meant what he said. Anna was going to be a part of his life and the sooner his mother came to terms with it the better for everyone.

Taking the stairs two at a time, Nick whistled, feeling hopeful and excited with his prospects where one Anna Blake was concerned.

～

SPAGHETTI.

That's what Anna felt like as she hobbled into the dimly lit meditation room with the soothing new-age music and hushed ambiance. She hadn't realized how tightly wound up she was until her entire body was placed under the thorough and unyielding hands of Brenda, her masseuse.

Anna stopped at the refreshment bar set up inside the entrance, topping off her peppermint tea that she wished were a triple vanilla latte as she looked around for a quiet, hidden space to decompress. Preferably one where her chatty sister wouldn't find her. The secret she'd learned this morning was weighing on her more than she liked and she didn't like the fact she knew something that, by all rights, Janie should know, too.

When had she become so protective of the spoiled princess who, at this time last week, had only inspired vague resentment and jealousy? Instead, Anna felt a swelling of affection and concern for the girl who she once thought had everything and now knew hadn't had such a charmed life after all.

Sinking into one of the gray chairs in the corner, she pulled her cell phone from the pocket of the soft ivory robe. There were a few emails from work and texts from both Quinn and Tessa checking in on her. She was in the middle of a chat with Tessa when the loud whispers and giggles from a couple of new arrivals stopped her.

She peered around a large vase of flowers to see Janie and Sara topping off their own beverages.

Had the woman no shame? Going on pretending that she was friends with Janie, that she had her interest at heart, when any time now Janie was going to discover the truth and feel like the rug was ripped out from under her feet.

Anna couldn't imagine doing to her two best friends what Sara had done to Janie. How could she watch Janie and Dax play the happy couple, walking hand-in-hand on the sunny beaches of Mexico, and then slip into his room later that night with no concern for how it would make Janie feel? Did she feel the slightest bit of guilt? If not then, maybe now as the moment of reckoning drew nearer?

"There you are," Janie said, her laser-like eyes homing in on Anna immediately. "They should be coming to get us any time now for our detoxifying seaweed body wrap. Nothing guarantees a girl relief from post-drinking body bloat like a detoxifying wrap, or so Mother always says."

"Janie? Anna?" Two women were standing at the entrance looking expectantly at them.

"And look at that timing. What'd I tell you?" Janie said. Turning to Sara, she added, "I'll catch up with you and the other girls for our mani-pedis. If we're running late, make sure everyone knows that we're going with the pearly petal pink polish."

"I'll do my best," Sara said and dropped into another chair, already pulling her phone out.

Anna and Janie followed their attendants down a couple of hallways until they reached the designated room, Janie keeping up a steady stream of conversation the entire time. Her high-spirited and angst-free mood was confirmation that, once again, Dax still hadn't found the time to make his big confession.

Was he even trying? And if he didn't...could Anna let Janie marry the guy without having all the facts? Lord, please let Dax come clean and save her from having to make that kind of decision.

It wasn't until after they were left alone, their seaweed-plastered bodies bundled tightly in hot towels, the lights turned down low as the magical wraps did their shrinkage, that Anna had the chance to prod Janie for any details. "Did you and Dax have a nice morning?"

"It was lovely. Coffee in bed, snuggled up together... I can't tell you how stressed I've been this week, and this morning was the first time in a long time we had a chance to slow down and take a deep breath and just be. Well, until our mothers decided to crash the party early."

Ah. Yes. The mothers. Their arrival would certainly have thrown a wrench in Dax's plan for a meaningful heart-to-heart. Especially Kathryn St. Claire.

Anna peeked over at Janie, who was lying, like her, on

her back in a mummified pose, her eyes closed. "How do you and Dax's mom get along?"

Janie laughed nervously. "Well, you know how it is. I'm taking her baby boy away. I try to give her the benefit of the doubt, but to be honest, I don't think she likes me very much."

Now it was Anna's turn to laugh. "You and I seem to have that in common. I wouldn't let it bother you. I think Kathryn enjoys making those around her uncomfortable, even those she likes. It makes her feel powerful."

"She definitely likes to makes an impression. Although I have to admit that I got a tiny bit of satisfaction in knowing that she never impressed Daddy. He trusted politicians as far as he could throw them, so he was less than excited to hear that I was getting married into a well-known political family like the St. Claires. Fortunately, Dax is so sweet and unassuming that Daddy couldn't help but love him. Well...at least think fondly of him."

Anna got a bit of her own satisfaction at knowing that, even though she didn't know Malcolm and doubted they would have gotten along, he hadn't let Kathryn get the better of him.

"Oh! I'm sorry, Anna, for going on about Daddy like that when I know how terribly he treated you, of all people." She paused. "If it makes you feel any better, I know he felt awful about not being part of your life."

"I doubt that, Janie."

"No, really. When the attorney told us the terms of the will and about you, he gave me a letter that Daddy wrote."

That got Anna's attention, but she tried to sound casual as she asked, "Oh, really?"

"It wasn't anything greeting-card-worthy or anything. Daddy wasn't like that; he always got right to the point, never mind niceties. He basically asked me to reach out to you, something that, in his life, he never could do. It was as close to saying he regretted that choice as he could get."

Anna processed this new information. He had wanted Janie to attempt to be a part of her life, even if he couldn't be. She didn't know how to feel about that, or if it was enough to feel anything. She hadn't been a poodle or a distant cousin. She'd been his daughter.

"Isn't that like me?" Janie said. "To get off the whole point of this conversation, which was that if either of us have an ounce of Daddy's bullishness, we wouldn't let Kathryn St. Claire push us around like she did to you today."

"You don't have to worry about me. That woman can't intimidate me. Not anymore."

"It's something of a miracle that Dax turned out as warm and loving and devoted as he did with her as his mother. From what I gathered from him and Nick, their dad was the more involved parent in their lives, taking them on camping trips and to basketball games and going to their swim meets, which made it so much harder on poor Dax when he died. Dax was only fifteen."

"That would be rough," she said.

But it was Nick who had Anna's mind churning. Knowing what she did about his dad's strong influence in their lives, his active participation with his sons, it had to have made it more devastating for Nick to discover his dad's infidelity. He was betrayed by the one parental figure in his life that he'd looked up to and wanted to emulate.

Not that she could share that with Janie. Nick had told her that in confidence, and as much as she was enjoying this moment of sharing, that was one confidence she was going to keep. What a mess family could be, with all their faults and human frailties.

"Anna?"

She opened an eye and looked over at Janie. "Yeah?"

"I'm so happy that you're in my life," Janie said sleepily. "Thank you for being here with me."

There was a lump in Anna's throat as she tried to swallow, her emotions too raw. "Me, too."

CHAPTER 15

NICK WATCHED Dax as he attempted to make the next shot, his head clearly not in the game despite the merriment of the other men. The guy was undoubtedly tied up in knots about the conversation he was going to have with his fiancée, and rightfully so.

When Nick discovered that his younger brother had been sleeping with both Janie and Sara in Mexico and had never come clean about it before setting Nick up with Sara, he'd been pissed as hell. Dax should have been up-front with Janie and Nick from the beginning.

It was just like Dax to think he wouldn't have to confront the error of his ways. His younger brother had jumped into things without worrying about the consequences of his actions his entire life, often not having to face the music because of some miraculous—or motherly—intervention.

But there was no miracle to be had here, and Dax was going to pay for his shortsightedness. Nick just hoped that it wouldn't be in a way that would cause long-term damage.

Like being left at the altar.

It was time Nick had it out with Dax. Enough was

enough. He didn't like seeing his brother so torn up, obviously needing someone to talk to about this. He waited until the guys were climbing into the golf cart to grab Dax. "Why don't you and I walk to the next hole. There is something I want to talk to you about."

"Okay," Dax said, appearing even more miserable.

They walked a minute while Nick wrestled with what to say. Dax took it on himself to speak first. "Nick, there's something I've been wanting to tell you for some time, something that's been eating away at me. It's about Sara."

Nick considered letting his brother squirm, to make him find the tough words that should have been spoken long ago, but he had mercy. He knew the hardest conversation was still to come. "Dax, I already know. About Mexico."

Dax paused mid-step. "Wait. You know? How? When?"

"I overheard you and Sara arguing about it last year, after you announced your engagement to Janie."

"Shit. I'm sorry, Nick. I didn't want you to find out like that. I don't know what I was thinking, not when I was with her or when I kept it from you and Janie...I screwed up."

"Yes, you did, and you screwed up this morning when you decided to have a repeat of that chat with Sara in the kitchen. Anna overheard."

Dax stared at him in horror. "You don't think she'll tell Janie?"

"Nah. She is going to give you the pleasure of doing that, as long as you do it soon. Which begs the question, why the hell did you wait so long?"

"I was scared shitless I'd lose her. Our relationship was so new; I didn't think it would take much to send her running. It wasn't like she didn't already have a ton of guys into her. I thought that with time, as we became more certain of each other, it would get easier to tell her, but I kept chickening out. Then, as you obviously heard, I was ready to after our engagement, but Sara made all those points about why it was best for both of us not to rehash the past and I buckled."

"You could have told me. Let me know what kind of a person I was getting involved with. It might have saved both her and me a lot of time."

"Yeah. I know, and I'm sorry. I really am. The thing that's ironic is that long ago I swore that once I found someone I cared about, I would never betray them or give them reason to doubt our love. And now...I'm just like him."

This time Nick nearly stumbled as he cast a glance at his brother. "Him?"

"Dad. You don't have to protect me from the truth, Nick. I figured it out a long time ago."

Nick looked incredulously at his brother, questions jumping out such as for how long had his brother known and how had he found out, but he realized they didn't have the time to delve into that now.

"Do you think Mom knew?" Dax asked.

"Well, considering the fact that both of her sons knew—and neither of us were particularly sleuth-like—it's a good assumption. She confirmed it for me today, in fact."

"She did? How did that come up?"

"When she was trying to tell me all the reasons I should consider marrying Sara, who would be my partner just as Mom was to Dad. Fidelity didn't seem that important to her." Up ahead, they could see the guys already in position, ready to tee off again. They didn't have much time. "So what now? Because as I see it, you're running out of opportunities to tell Janie the truth. The wedding is tomorrow."

"I know, it's just that every time I tried today, something came up. I will. I'm just glad I no longer have to worry about how this is going to affect you, affect us, because I owe you so much, man. I'm sorry I didn't tell you sooner."

"It's all right. Just do the right thing. And grovel. A lot."

"Speaking of groveling... You and Anna seem to have reached some sort of truce yourselves. You know, if things work out the way I'm hoping with Janie, we could always try and do the whole Brady double wedding thing. Mom would love it."

Nick chuckled at that image, but he quickly sobered at the thought of standing next to Anna, saying he was ready to commit to her for the rest of their lives.

It didn't sound so funny anymore.

WHILE JAKE GAVE a rambling toast to the happy couple—clearly imbibing more of the wine than the food—Anna studied the room where tonight's rehearsal dinner was being held, still in awe of the transformation that Lorenzo had given the wine cellar in one day.

It was better than she'd hoped.

Candles and pendant lighting warmed the dark recesses of the subterranean room. Linens as red as the burgundy wine in the glasses and peonies and roses in white and pink covered the tables. The vibe was romantic, the heady aroma of tonight's food was enticing, and the best man sitting next to her...intoxicating.

It had been jarring seeing him again at the church after having spent hours thinking about him thanks to too much downtime at the spa. It had helped her put things in perspective. About their history, about his so-called charmed existence growing up a St. Claire, and, most particularly, about how quickly she was discovering she cared about him and wanted the best for him.

No, how she wanted...him.

Not that she could tell him that. She was grateful she hadn't done anything stupid when their eyes met for the briefest moment as she walked down the aisle during the rehearsal and a rush of crazy emotions flooded her.

But here, right now, his arm just a few inches from hers, his fingers clasping the stem of his water glass as he kept his eyes trained on Jake, she was aware of every detail about him. The jagged edges of his cuticles. The way he rubbed his fingers over his chin when he was deep in thought. The way his bottom lip puckered in in the middle as if inviting someone to tease it with their tongue. The heat that seemed to emanate from his skin that made her want to reach out and touch him and feel its warmth.

All combined gave her a heady, giddy feeling.

Raising her gaze, she caught sight of another person who appeared to be studying...her. With her silvery-gray hair, a teal-colored shawl that complemented her coloring, and a calm aura about her, the woman was the epitome of elegance and beauty. Probably close to her late sixties, the woman was seated next to Elise Van Hollins, who, thankfully, along with Kathryn St. Claire, was seated at a separate table this evening.

Anna wondered who the woman was and why she had attracted her attention. Nervously, Anna pulled her gaze away and brought it back to Jake, who was wrapping up his story, encouraged by the audience's applause.

"Everything all right?" Nick asked near her ear, his breath a whisper that tickled the sensitive skin under her lobe.

Even though she hadn't said anything or thought she'd

acted any differently, he'd picked up on her unease. "Just a lot more people around tonight who I don't know."

His arm moved closer to hers, subtly, so that their forearms were nearly touching. Then his pinky stretched the last inch until it touched her.

"You belong here, Anna. Don't doubt that for a minute."

His voice was like butter, and she was instantly comforted. She risked a glance at him and was nearly undone by the warmth in those dark eyes. Not just warmth, but need. For her.

She swallowed. Her heart was beating loud and fast, and she took a breath to calm it. He'd grown bolder and covered her hand with his, the gentleness of his fingertips across the top of her hand mesmerizing her.

"Anna, Nick," Janie said loudly enough to have Anna pulling her hand away from Nick. "I can't thank you two enough for finding this place. It's exactly what I wanted for tonight. Inviting, relaxed, and so romantic," she said, tucking her arm into Dax's, who was sitting on her other side. "I especially can't wait until Dax and I can get away to find a certain apple tree I hear is positively magical."

Dear God. She hadn't just said that.

What had Anna been thinking when she confided that intimate detail with Janie after showering the remnants of the seaweed mixture from their bodies and taking a few minutes to sit in the sauna together? The peppermint tea must have been drugged. That's it.

"Magical, huh?" Nick asked and returned his hand to hers, this time capturing both Dax's and Janie's attention.

She couldn't look at him. "I don't remember putting it exactly like that."

"I think I'm missing something," Dax said.

"Don't worry, baby. I'll fill you in as soon as we can get

away for our own little magic," Janie said and nuzzled his jaw.

The moment was broken when a new voice rose above the din, another offering of a toast to the future bride and groom. Sara.

Anna looked at Dax, whose face seemed to have drained of blood, while Janie leaned forward in anticipation of what her friend might say.

Anna held her breath.

"Janie was a worldly thirteen years old that day she caught sight of the worldlier fourteen-year-old Dax," Sara said, smiling easily. "Over a late-night campfire with s'mores and hot chocolate, the two of them decided they were meant for each other. Over the years, as they both grew older and wiser, they also grew apart. But the moment they set eyes on each other that night in Mexico, nearly ten years later, they both swore that the years melted away and, once again, they only had eyes for each other. Or at least, that's how they've told it all these years."

Sara paused, and her gaze fell on Dax, an unspoken message passing to him. A warning. A reminder of the eloquent words he'd claimed at their engagement party that Janie wouldn't find so romantic and heartfelt, especially once she learned he'd slipped away only hours after their reunion to spend the night with Janie's best friend.

"And now, two years later, we're finally going to see the real-life fairy tale of their love come true as they get married. I'm sure all of us would like to raise our glasses again to wish our best to the happy couple on the eve of their wedding." She raised her glass. "To true love."

Man. She was good.

Anna glanced over to Janie, who beamed at her friend before kissing Dax loudly on the cheek.

"Thank you, Sara," Janie said, having risen to her feet. "You've always been such a good friend and I'm so happy you could be here today. That all of you could be here. I know that tomorrow is going to be absolutely perfect, just like my love for Dax." More oohing and aahing as everyone raised their glasses again. "So, please, feel free to relax and enjoy another glass of wine or more of this delicious food. There's also a table filled with chocolate temptations waiting up the stairs if you care to hang out a little longer, or maybe take a walk under the stars. I'll see you all tomorrow. I'll be the girl in white."

It was the cue people seemed to be waiting for as many of them rose, taking a second to shake hands, give hugs, and move around to speak to those they might not have had a chance to before.

Nick stood, too, buttoning his dinner jacket as he did. "I'll be right back. I need to go speak with Sara. Will you be okay?"

What on earth could he say to Sara that would make any of this better? But she didn't ask, just nodded. It appeared that Janie and Dax had also slipped away, something that brought Anna a sense of relief. The dinner had at least reached its end before disaster, though the knot of anxiety in Anna's stomach made her question what was still to come.

If she was worried she wouldn't have anyone to talk to, she could have saved herself the concern, for the older woman who'd been studying her before sank into Janie's seat and positioned her shawl around her. Jasmine. She smelled of jasmine and...honeysuckle.

"Good evening, dear," she said and raised her blue eyes to Anna's, an easy smile on her feathery-thin lips. "You must be my niece, Anna. I would know those Van Hollins eyes and those cheekbones anywhere. I'm Lenore, Malcolm's sister. I'm happy to finally meet you."

This was the woman who used to bring Janie cotton-candy-flavored jelly beans and take her to the Space Needle and the carousel in the park? Anna felt a sudden strange sense of loss at not having the same opportunity.

"Not that I wouldn't have enjoyed meeting you sooner," she continued, not waiting for Anna's response. "But I was told in no uncertain terms that Rachel was raising you alone and my interference was the last thing anyone needed. Although I may not have been actively involved in your life, I did follow your progress all these years."

"You knew about me?" Anna asked in surprise.

"I did. I was fond of your mother back when she and Malcolm were together and was disappointed when they ended things. Rachel always liked her independence and Malcolm needed someone who...well, needed him. Rachel certainly did not."

That about summed up her mother.

The old woman continued to study Anna's face. "I am glad to finally make your acquaintance, Anna. I hope you'll give us the chance to get to know each other."

"I...I would like that." Oddly enough, she meant it. Coming into this thing, she'd had no intention of having a relationship with any of these people. Her purpose was to get in here, do her time and get the story, and get back out, returning to her normally scheduled life.

Then, little by little, she'd found herself opening up thanks to a sweet but pushy and somewhat needy younger sister, not to mention an enigmatic man who made her see everything from a different perspective. He opened her eyes so she could appreciate her past and the people who'd made her who she was, for better or worse.

"I'm glad to hear that. I didn't know what you'd say when you met me. I half feared you might tell me go to hell and you would have been completely entitled. I'm glad that you're far more clear-headed than me."

Anna managed a smile, but something the woman said was niggling at her. "You mentioned that you'd been following my progress? How do you mean?"

The woman pursed her lips in a secretive smile. "Let's just say I have a lot of friends in San Francisco, friends with influence, who kept me apprised of your progress. And when that little kerfuffle between you and the St. Claire boy came up, I might have had a hand in making sure you were equally represented at the school's disciplinary board." She looked over at Kathryn, who was speaking to a few older men Anna didn't recognize. "Kathryn St. Claire always did have too high of an opinion of herself."

Anna didn't know how to react. She was stunned. She supposed she should feel grateful for her interference, if what she said was true, but instead, she felt even more cheated. If this woman cared, why hadn't she made her presence known then? God knew that Anna could have used an ally back then. She loved her mother and was very proud of all that Rachel had accomplished, but she was busy with her work and Anna's life had been, at times, lonely.

"I guess I owe you a thanks."

"Please. That was the least I could do and you very well know it. Now, I can see that the passage of time has changed a few things, not the least of which is your feelings where the St. Claire boy is concerned. He's really quite the charmer. He reminds me a bit of my late husband."

How could she even know this? It wasn't like she or Nick had been flirting or kissing. Heck, they'd barely touched in the space of time they'd sat next to each other. Were her feelings that obvious to everyone?

A sudden rising inexplicable panic gripped her.

Air. Anna needed air.

"As much as I'd like to catch up, I'm supposed to be helping with the dessert table if you'll excuse me."

"Of course," the older woman said, her eyes too understanding.

Anna pushed away from the table and looked for the stairs and the way up and out of the suddenly suffocating atmosphere of the room.

The cold Napa night air was a welcome sensation from the earlier heat, and she gasped in its sharpness.

There was a burning sense of emotion thrumming through her that she hadn't previously recognized. Anger, frustration, and incredible sadness.

Emotions directed at a father who'd abandoned her and who she couldn't confront since he was gone, but she also could recognize anger that she'd been holding on to for her mother.

Rachel had been independent. Stubbornly so. If she had relinquished some of that independence, especially with regard to rearing her daughter, what would Anna's life have been like? Would she have known Janie? Lenore? Maybe even Malcolm?

A hot tear slipped down her cheek and she wiped it away.

She'd always felt rejected by her family. Unwanted. Not worthy. Could things have been different?

From behind her, a warm hand rested on her shoulder and she looked up to find Nick staring at her in concern. "Hey. You okay? What happened?"

"I...I just needed to catch my breath is all."

Only, for some crazy reason, the tears she'd held back were flooding her eyes and raining down her cheeks, and she strangled back a sob.

It was mortifying.

But instead of appearing disgusted or embarrassed by her show of emotion, Nick's face was one of concern as he came forward and wrapped his arm around her.

"Come on. Let's get out of here. My car is around back."

Thank God. There was no way she was going to be able to stop this torrent of tears in time to board the bus. The last thing she wanted was to have to explain her breakdown.

"Here." Without even asking, Nick was shrugging off his jacket and placing it around her shoulders.

Instantly, she was blanketed in its warm, protective softness that smelled distinctly like Nick. She instinctively brought it tighter around her.

Needing the comfort. The familiarity.

Knowing that, for the first time, she was with someone who really cared.

Against her will, a fresh bout of tears appeared.

CHAPTER 16

NICK KNEW THAT, for the moment, Anna needed to let the emotions that overwhelmed her play out, so he didn't try to get her to talk to him on the quick ride back to the estate, even if the sound of the tears that choked her up was making concentration difficult.

He hated seeing her so upset, especially since he knew that this display was probably costing her a lot. Anna didn't seem like a woman who easily cried.

The empty quiet of the house as they walked inside was a welcome change from the night's revelries. In continued silence, they climbed the stairs and headed toward their rooms.

This night wasn't going exactly how he'd planned. He had hoped to bank on the romantic ambiance of the night's venue, maybe find that tree again that she had thought so magical.

"Thank you for getting me out of there," she said as they reached her door, the first time she'd spoken since leaving the restaurant. She slid his jacket off and handed it back to him. "And thank you for this."

He tucked it under his arm. "Of course."

She opened her door, appearing like she was ready to disappear inside and withdraw into her solitude and sadness for the night, something he couldn't let happen.

"Wait. Anna. Tell me what happened. Maybe talking about it will make you feel better."

"There isn't much to say. I got overwhelmed with emotion and I'm embarrassed about the whole thing. Nothing that a good night's sleep won't solve."

"Come on. You and I both know that there's no chance you're going to go in there and instantly fall to sleep. Not when you have so much on your mind. Have I ever told you what an excellent listener I am?"

She hesitated, as if considering letting him in.

"Besides, I didn't get to tell you about my chat with Dax earlier."

That seemed to have done the trick. And trick was what it was since there really wasn't much to tell. But he was inside, meaning he'd earned the chance to spend a little more time with her.

Anna crossed the room to the window and sank onto the small chaise that looked like a match to the one in his room. He sat on the corner of the bed. "So what exactly happened?" he asked softly. "When I left the table, you seemed to be doing okay." His mind latched on to a possibility he hadn't considered before. "It wasn't my mother, was it? Did she say something to you?" A string of curses crossed his mind at what the woman could have said that would bring the type of reaction he'd witnessed. She didn't learn, and if she—

"No. It wasn't her. I met my aunt Lenore." She smiled, trying to sound happy, but her tone was strained. "After all these years believing I had no family who loved me or wanted to know me, it turned out that maybe I was wrong."

Nick knew Lenore, she'd been at the engagement party when she'd seemed harmless enough. Pretty and charming —very much like her niece—but he'd clearly gotten that wrong if, on meeting her, Anna was like this. "What did she say to you?"

"She told me how much she had wanted to know me, but because of my parents' selfish reasons, she didn't get a chance. Those are my words."

There was an edge of bitterness in her tone, and he waited patiently for her to continue.

She stood abruptly, pacing in front of him. "For all these years, my entire life, Malcolm was all too happy to wash his hands of the responsibility for me. Just when I had accepted that and moved on, he goes and dies, leaving a letter to Janie asking her to reach out to me. What the heck is up with that? I mean, if you're going to pretend someone doesn't exist their entire life and that person has now adjusted to that, you don't mess with the status quo and try to build something that's probably too late. And don't get me started on my mother." Anna paused, pulling at her hair for a minute. "Rachel, who always had to have her independence. To hell with what the cost of that independence would be on her daughter, a daughter who was left to her own devices for most of her life. She thought it would toughen me up and help me realize I didn't need anyone but myself. She didn't care if I spent every Thanksgiving alone in front of the TV with a pizza delivered from around the corner, or my birthday staring at a handwritten note offering me a rain check for dinner when she got back from Zimbabwe. No one ever asked me what I wanted."

"What do you want, Anna?" he asked calmly.

She stopped, her eyes wild as they settled on him, and she seemed to catch her breath. "I just want to be someone's first choice for once. For someone not to take the easy way out of getting to know me because they were given permission not to. For someone to choose to cut their trip short to be there for my birthday because they thought that, maybe, I was more important. All I want is for someone to actually choose...me. Put me first."

Another tear slipped from her cheek, and his heart tightened at the thought that anyone would think she wasn't worthy of being their number one.

He stood, walking slowly toward her until he was close enough to wipe the tear from her face with his thumb. Close enough that when her eyes shut at the touch, he could wrap her into his arms, holding her close to him, letting her know without words that he would be there for her.

He wasn't going anywhere.

A calming energy fell over him as he accepted this truth. Knowing with certainty that in the space of a few days, this woman had become the person he was meant to be there for. Meant to love.

Anna stayed rigid in his arms for another moment before finally accepting the comfort he was offering. Her body slowly softened and she melted into him. Trusting him.

"I'm sorry," he said. "I'm sorry that anyone ever made you feel like you weren't important. That you weren't the most precious thing in their life. Because you are worthy of having someone love you like that. Someone who appreciates how wonderful you are. Someone who can see everything you have to offer them."

"Yeah? Like what?" she asked, her face buried against him and making it hard to hear her words.

He smiled. "Well, for one, your biting but infectious charm."

He felt her smile against his shoulder. "Go on."

"You have a smile that lights up the area around you and makes a man think he's staring at an angel."

She chuckled now. "An angel. Right."

"I'm just repeating what Lorenzo said," he teased, reminding her of the old Italian's words. "Let's see. What else... You're also persistent in getting what you want."

"And that's a good thing?"

"It is. I know that when you set your sights on something, you'll never give up. Then there are the more obvious traits that right now, holding you this close to me, are becoming harder for me not to be aware of." Like the softness of her breasts that he'd already been appreciating all night as they pushed up against the slinky black number she wore. "Have I told you yet just how amazing you look in that dress?"

This time she pulled away and laughed as she met his gaze. "Always a one-track mind."

"I told you it's my soundtrack playing softly in the background. Lately, though, only when I'm around you."

And bam. Like that, the humor of the moment dissipated and they were left staring at each other, her blue eyes wide with understanding and something even better.

Mutual desire.

Her gaze dropped to his mouth, which was probably a mistake since he'd barely been holding on to his control before, but with her pressed against him like this, staring at him like she wanted to feel his lips against hers, he felt the last vestige of control slip away.

Greedily, he dipped his head to taste the sweet softness of her mouth, to tease her tongue with his until she opened her mouth more fully to his. Her back arched up as if she was trying to get closer to him, and he took a few steps back until they reached the wall, somewhere he could lean against that would support them both from the deluge of emotions and passion making him as weak as it was strong.

Only it wasn't enough. For either of them.

"Anna." He waited until she opened her eyes and focused on him. The smoky gaze of passion nearly undid him. "Before we get more carried away, I want you to tell me that this is what you want, because God knows that you are all I want. Not just tonight either. So I need you to know that if we do this, I'm not going to let you walk back out of my life like the other guys in your life. I'm sticking around. Forever."

Her breath hitched, and she stared at him in surprise.

"Anna. You're the most incredibly maddening and exciting woman I've ever known. You have a bad habit of getting under my skin and not letting go. Not now, and not ten years ago."

She reached up to slide her hand through his hair, as if in disbelief that he was standing here now, telling her these things. "I think I've always wanted this. Always wanted you, too."

"Then if you're on board with this," he said and smiled, "with us, I'm going to show you in excruciating detail exactly how beautiful and wonderful you are."

"Promise?" she asked, returning his smile, which was the sign he'd been waiting for.

Taking care not rush the moment, he slipped his fingers under the straps of her dress and slid the gauzy material down inch by inch. Her hands joined his, her need and anticipation matching his, until they were standing together with nothing between them but hope and excitement and always that little bit of fear.

This was what he'd been waiting for his entire life.

This moment. This woman. This night.

And he proceeded to show her just that, in painfully slow and toe-curling movement that made the waiting all worthwhile.

THE MORNING SUN hadn't yet crept into her room when Anna slowly came awake, aware of the man next to her. Instead of the gripping cold fear that often happened when she found herself in the position of being with a guy that she might have feelings for, Anna didn't feel fear. Or regret. Or an insatiable need to creep out of bed and sneak away before things got too real.

So this was what it was like. To love someone. To know they matched that love with their own even if the words hadn't been spoken. He'd said enough with every touch and whisper of adoration.

Her heart was full as she turned her head to watch him sleep for a few more minutes.

She would stay here like this forever if she could, but there were other things she had to finish before the start of the day, like a certain story she'd promised would be in her editor's mailbox by the end of the night.

Leaning down, she kissed Nick's soft lips, lingering over them for a second.

His eyes opened slowly to stare at her, and a languid smile tugged on his lips. "Morning. What time is it?"

"Time for me to get the finishing touches finalized on that feature story of a certain up-and-coming state senator."

Nick stretched his arms overhead and then quickly wrapped them around her, flipping her over to her back. "Are you sure you want to bury yourself in something as dry and boring as that? I can think of something infinitely more interesting we can bury ourselves in," he said, nuzzling against her throat.

She let him kiss her, enjoying the feeling of his weight on top of her, the delicious feeling of his arms surrounding her, his lips expertly moving to that area under her ear that made everything slip away—

No. She needed a clear head.

She laughed and pushed him away. "You are not going to distract me. Not this time. I have work to do."

He grinned. "It was worth a try."

She watched him dress without trying to hide her appreciation as he pulled his clothes on. "I guess it's probably best that I sneak away to my own room before someone catches us and gets the house buzzing about something other than the wedding."

That's right, it was today. "Wait, didn't you tell me you had a chat with Dax? He was still planning on telling Janie everything, right?"

"He was, which means that I probably should get out there and ready for whatever the day brings us." Fully clothed, he sat back on the bed and leaned over, cupping his hand behind her head to pull her in for another kiss. "Meet me in my room in an hour. We can go down to breakfast together, unless you need more time for your story."

"An hour is fine. I'm just tying up a few things."

He stood again and crossed the room, turning at the door to look at her. "All right. Just remember. You're not getting rid of me now. You're stuck with me. Forever."

She didn't know what was more surprising to her. That he'd said it...or that she believed him.

THERE WAS the sound of pounding. Nonstop pounding.

Nick groaned and rolled over, trying to drown out the sound. It took him another moment to realize that the sound was coming from his door, and another second to realize that someone wasn't going to stop pounding before he threw his covers off and sat up.

Shit. He'd meant to close his eyes for a minute after his shower but he must have fallen asleep.

Anna.

Immediately, the last remnants of fatigue disappeared. He grabbed his pants and slid them on and picked up a tee shirt, which he pulled over his head as he answered the door. "I hope that you— Mother." He closed his eyes and counted to three, forcing himself to be patient with the woman standing pristinely dressed as always in navy tailored slacks and a white blouse. "Please tell me you're not here to give me another lecture about my responsibilities."

"Do you really not know what's going on?" Kathryn St. Claire asked, pushing her way in without waiting for an invitation. "What on earth do you pay your communications people for at that office of yours? They should have had a hold on this by now."

He yawned and took a moment to glance out at the hallway to see if Anna was on her way, but the hall was silent since most rational people were still in bed sleeping. "Slow down," he said and shut his door behind him. "What's this morning's crisis?"

"Why don't you read the headlines yourself." She held her phone out to him.

With reluctance, especially as he caught the look on his mother's face—angry, no doubt, but also gloating—he took her phone and scanned the screen, noting it came from *The Daily Rundown*'s breaking news section posted thirty minutes ago.

Rumors of Affairs rock the St. Claire family.

What the hell? He sat down on the bed as he read through the sludge.

Multiple sources have confirmed that the late US Senator Richard St. Claire engaged in several long-term affairs during his marriage to Kathryn St. Claire, and it appears that his youngest son, Dax St. Claire, who is to be married today to millionaire heiress Janie Van Hollins, is following in his father's footsteps as new sources point to the younger's indiscretions while dating Ms. Van Hollins.

The clincher of the story was in the next paragraph.

Will these rumors threaten Nick St. Claire's state senate campaign that he was scheduled to announce next week?

It felt like someone had kicked him in the gut and, when he'd fallen to the ground, given him a couple more kicks for good measure. Everything that was being said, about Janie and Dax, his impending campaign, his parents...none of this was common knowledge. He scrolled back up to read the byline.

Staff writer. He felt a moment's relief despite the dark cloud festering overhead.

"I told you that getting mixed up with that woman again was going to bring you nothing but grief, Nicholas," his mother continued. She was leaning against the wall by the window, her arms folded in front of her. "Now she's about to destroy everything that your father has built, your political legacy, not to mention Dax's marriage, to further her own career."

"Mother, we have no idea where this story came from. There are any number of people who could have shared this. Anyone here—"

"How many people here know the details about your father's infidelity? Or that Sara and Dax once had an affair? Or about your upcoming campaign? Are you telling me that Anna didn't know about these things?"

He clenched his teeth together. "It's possible that Sara knew all these things. Your calling her the other day was like waving a red flag in front of her that something was going on, politically speaking. It wouldn't have been too hard for her to make the right calls and figure it out."

"And why would Sara do that? What would she gain?" Kathryn asked calmly. "Right now, if anyone stood to look the worse here, it's Sara for sleeping with her best friend's guy and jeopardizing that friendship."

"If it's not Sara, there must be another possibility."

"Face it, Nicholas. There's only one person who knew all those details and who had the most to gain."

He tried to fight the sinking feeling in his gut, a sinking he'd felt so many time before. Each time denying what was in front of him until the evidence became clear.

Not just with Sara. There was Kristie, his first high school girlfriend who had, it turned out, been dating him while angling for a spot as an intern at his dad's office to pump up her Princeton college application. There was Tanya, his college girlfriend who was trying to get her fashion blog off the ground and hoped that the attention she got from dating Nick would catapult her to success. There had been a few other posers, women and men, who'd tried to use a romance or friendship with him to further their own interests.

But Anna? She wasn't like everyone else. She was different.

There had to be another explanation.

Okay, he could think this through. Rationally. Objectively. What would Anna have to gain? She would have to know that running this story would ruin any chance she had at having a relationship with not just him, but with Janie, too.

Then again, she'd come into this week with one purpose: to get the story that would save her career. Maybe even make it. And the story he'd been prepared to give her would have saved it, but this one...definitely could make it.

His mother seemed to sense his inner battle and softened her posture as she came to stand next to him, placing her hand on his shoulder. "I know this isn't easy for you, and it's not going to be easy for Dax. We need to stick together, keep our heads up, and limit our interaction with the press until after today's ceremony that I can only pray will go on as scheduled. Then, first thing Monday, we'll talk tactics and what kind of official statement we want to give."

"I should go and check on Dax and see if he knows about all of this yet," Nick said, his voice sounding calmer than he felt. But with the calmness, there was numbness, too. Something he welcomed until he could clear the fog in his brain. "Hopefully he did what he set out to do last night and told Janie everything about him and Sara, and this story won't be a shock to Janie."

His mother walked to the door and opened it. "If that young woman knows what's good for her, she'll have left the house and saved us all from a painful and unnecessary confrontation."

Left? Nick looked at the time. It was already twenty minutes past the time Anna was supposed to have come and met him. Had she left, hoping to avoid a confrontation?

No, he wouldn't jump to conclusions. He couldn't. Not after everything they'd come to mean to each other, after everything they'd promised each other. She couldn't have been faking all of that.

For the time being, he'd try and do damage control. Make sure there was still a wedding.

Then he'd deal with Anna.

CHAPTER 17

ANNA KNOCKED on Nick's door for the second time and paused. She couldn't hear anything on the other side. She'd gotten so caught up in the story, adding another nuance that she hoped would make Nick more down-to-earth, that she'd lost track of the time, only realizing she was late when she hit send.

He'd probably already gone down to join the party. She'd meet him there.

Her phone buzzed in her pocket and she saw that her editor had left another message for her. Charlie likely hadn't seen her email and was now in a panic that Anna wasn't going to uphold the agreement about getting the story to her tonight. Anna pocketed the phone, not in the mood to have to deal with her right now.

All she wanted to do was talk to Nick.

She smiled, remembering a few things about last night, things that had surprised them both. Maybe, if things were calm enough, they could sneak away for another private interlude.

As she reached the bottom of the stairs, she could hear

voices coming from the dining room, where everyone was congregating for breakfast. As she drew nearer, it was hard to mistake the shouts of anger from the other room.

She sighed. At least Dax had finally been honest and she didn't have to hide anything from anyone anymore.

Anna didn't expect the hush of silence that fell over the room as she stepped in, or the angry, accusatory glares directed her way.

"Good morning?" she said, growing uneasy from the animosity that seemed to be directed her way.

She spotted Janie sitting down, with Trish and Megan on either side of her. It was her sister's face that set off the alarm bells in her head. Red and splotchy from tears, she stood when she saw Anna.

"I thought you really cared about me," she said, anguish in her voice. "That you were actually here to try and build a relationship with me. But in the end, you were only playing a part. Pretending to care."

Anna froze, not expecting to hear the accusation. How had Janie found out about her agreement with Nick? Who would have told her?

She tried to figure out a response, something to assure Janie that her feelings for her sister were genuine. But she couldn't lie either, instead she needed her to understand. "Janie, I can explain. When I made that deal with Nick to play the part as your maid of honor, I—"

"Agreement with Nick? What are you talking about?" Janie's horror made it obvious that this wasn't what she had meant. "Never mind. I don't know if I want to know anything more. But answer me this. Why couldn't you come to me first and tell me in person what Dax and Sara had been doing behind my back? Wasn't I owed before you sold us all out to that rag you work for? Humiliating me, my family, Dax, his parents? Not to mention Nick."

Wait. What was she talking about? "What story?"

Janie's eyes filled with tears again. "Please. Stop the lies. The pretense."

"Janie, why don't you and I go talk somewhere quiet," Anna said, desperate to get away from the censure and anger from every person in that room.

"Whatever you have to say you can say here, among my friends."

It was like she'd entered the Twilight Zone. Where was Nick? Maybe he could help her make sense of this. "Look, I don't know what story you're talking about. Yes, when I first got here I wasn't exactly sold on the idea of stepping into the shoes of the maid of honor. In fact I only came here because my editor gave me no choice, not if I wanted to save my job. And Nick, well, he saw through it and we worked out another deal instead. He'd give me a story provided I pretend to be having a good time, doing everything that a maid of honor should do."

"So you were pretending all along to actually care about me."

That wasn't what she meant to say, but nothing was coming out right. She tried again. "No. I wasn't pretending. The more I got to know you, the more I found that I liked you and cared for you, which made it all the harder when I heard Dax and Sara talking about their affair—"

"So you knew about them." The flood of tears had stopped, and Janie looked at her with such hatred that Anna took a step back. "Even though you knew my best friend had screwed my fiancé and they'd been lying to me, you didn't think to come and tell me in person. How long, Anna? How long did you know about Dax and Sara?"

"Only since yesterday morning. I promise. I wanted to tell you, but Dax was going to tell you himself, and I thought I owed him the chance—"

"The chance to come clean before you wrote all the dirty details about us in this morning's news story?"

Again with the story. "Janie, I really don't know what you're talking about. My story that I've been working on with Nick's blessing isn't going to be published until tomorrow."

Megan stood to put her arm around Janie. "Well, then I suggest you read the breaking news story that your company published. Maybe it will enlighten you. Then, I think it would be a good idea that you go. Your being here right now is not making anything easier for Janie to process."

This was from the same woman who Anna had shared a mimosa with after their hot air balloon adventure yesterday, feeling like maybe, just maybe, she did belong and that these people could be her friends, too. Trish had joined Megan in flanking their friend, as they led Janie from the room.

Her head pounding, Anna pulled out her phone, trying to see through a blur in front of her eyes that put everything out of focus. What was going on? What was this story that everyone was blaming her for?

It only took her a second to push the homepage for *The Daily Rundown*, and another second to scroll down and see the headline that had her finding a chair to sink into, her legs too wobbly to hold her up as she read the story.

How did they get this information? Who was this anonymous source?

Charlie. She'd been trying to reach her and now Anna had some suspicions as to why.

She was about to push redial to get her editor on the phone when she heard male voices coming into the room and she nearly wept in relief. "Nick," she said, coming to her feet. "Dax. This is all so crazy. I don't know how Charlie found out all that stuff for the story."

"Dax, you should go find Janie and try to talk to her," Nick said when he saw her, his face devoid of the smiles and warmth from earlier.

Dear God. Why was he looking at her like that? Cold. Almost empty.

She was aware of Dax leaving the room but she couldn't take her gaze from Nick's to tell if Dax was looking at her the same way as everyone else. Accusingly.

"Nick? Tell me you don't believe I had anything to do with this."

"I can't talk to you about this right now, Anna. Not yet."

She stood her ground, needing to know if everything she'd come to believe about this man, about his feelings for her, had been a lie. "You can and you will because I've done nothing wrong here. I had nothing to do with that story."

He sighed deeply, running his hands over his face, his first sign of emotion. "I want to believe you. I do. I just can't get away from the fact that you're the only person outside my family who knew all of the details that made their way into the story. About my upcoming campaign, about Dax and Sara, and even about my dad."

She fought back tears of rage at the injustice of it all, but she'd cried enough last night that she was all dried up. Yet the rage inside her still burned, fueling her forward. "You think I'd sell you out to impress my editor?"

"I don't know what you want me to say here, Anna. Do I think it's possible that you would do what you needed to protect yourself and your livelihood? To make enough of an impression that you would be sailing into a new, primo spot writing features at *The Rundown* or anywhere else you might want? Maybe."

Everything inside her felt like it was dying. All the hope and happiness from a few short minutes ago shriveled away. She turned away, unable to bear seeing the way he was looking at her. To see the doubt and disappointment he couldn't disguise.

"Hell, this is why I didn't want to talk to you about this right now. I don't know my own thoughts, much less anyone else's." He sounded anguished. "What we need to focus on right now is Janie and Dax and the wedding that's supposed to take place this evening. We need to make sure Janie realizes that not walking down that aisle to marry the man we all know she's meant to be with would be a mistake."

She laughed bitterly. "Do we? Do we all know they were meant to be? He lied to her all this time. What kind of marriage would that be if they can't trust each other? You know, if anything, they're probably better off finding out now, before they make a mistake they can't walk back from."

Anna was tired, so dang tired she could sink to the floor.

Nick claimed he couldn't think about whether she was guilty of selling everyone out for the sake of the story, but the truth was written on his face. In the way he couldn't quite meet her eye without blinking and looking away.

The last thing she wanted to do was fight for something that obviously wasn't right. If Nick wanted to believe the worst, she wasn't going to talk him out of it. She could stand here and explain all the reasons she wouldn't have done this until she was blue in the face, but the thing was, if he knew her as he'd claimed to, she wouldn't have to.

"I should go. My presence is only causing everyone added grief they don't need right now."

She'd save herself the pain of hearing him tell her that he chose to believe the lie instead of believing her, and end things on her terms.

At the door, she stopped, not trusting herself to look at him again. "I hope that everything works out for Janie, because, whether you believe it or not, I only want the best for her. For her to be happy." She hesitated. "For you, too."

Somehow she managed to hold the tears back until she reached the solace of her bedroom, very aware that Nick never followed.

ANNA STOOD on the front porch hiding behind the small potted tree and tried to look past the hordes of media vans and reporters parked outside the front gates to the Van Hollins estate.

Her Uber driver should have been here two minutes ago.

She hoped that she could hold off the angry crowd back in the house, and the clamoring reporters outside the house, until she could make it to the sanctity of the car that would take her to Tessa's family farm in Sonoma unscathed.

She cursed her editor for refusing to give up the name of the source who had provided the damaging information on the St. Claires. Charlie had held fast to maintaining his or her anonymity, particularly since she had personally verified the information with two other independent sources in the twelve hours she had from the time the tip came in until the time they went to press.

Viewership on the website had more than tripled its usual rate and that was in the first hour alone, which was the only thing that mattered to Charlie—not the fact that, in publishing the piece, she'd screwed over her own reporter, who was left to face the angry hordes unprepared.

The burning threat of tears surfaced again but Anna fought them. Not yet. Not here. Not when someone could see the shame and humiliation, the pain and the frustration that threatened to rip her apart.

The front door creaked open, and Anna's heart pounded as she waited to see who it was. Did they know she was out here? Was someone going to call over one of the security officers to escort her off the property? It would be the final blow to her dignity.

Lenore peered out, her gaze resting on Anna. "There you are. I was hoping I hadn't missed you."

The woman's voice was whispery soft and friendly, as were her eyes as she slipped out, shutting the door behind her. If the woman was angry, her demeanor didn't give it away, and Anna held her breath as she waited for what she had to say.

"It's such a shame that you're leaving so soon. We never had a chance to chat."

Anna didn't know how to respond. Hadn't her aunt been clued in to what was going on inside? "Yeah, well, I think it's best for everyone's sake that I make myself scarce."

"You'll forgive me if I disagree with you on that one. Nothing ever got resolved by running away."

Anna bristled at the shot. "I'm not running away. I just see no point in sticking around when it's been made clear that my presence is unwanted."

The older woman didn't say anything as she looked down, clutching her hands behind her back. "I see. May I ask where you're going? Back to the city?"

"No. My friend is out visiting her family in Sonoma. I'll head there for now."

"Ah, yes. Tessa Montenegro, I believe."

Anna looked at her sharply. "How do you know that?"

"I already told you. I have always kept a close eye on you."

"You'll forgive me for saying this, but that sounds kind of...stalkerish."

Lenore laughed. "Yes, I suppose it would. So is that who you're waiting for now? Tessa?"

Anna glanced out front again, trying to see if her car had arrived, before shaking her head. "I called for an Uber ride. They should be here any minute. In fact, I probably should meet them at the road. I wouldn't want them to get scared away by all the press."

"I don't suppose there's anything I could say that might make you reconsider leaving?"

"Not a chance. People believe what they want to believe, so who am I to argue with them? It doesn't matter to me either way."

"No?" Lenore studied Anna, her expression one of disappointment. Then she nodded. "Well, you have to do what's right for you. Remember, sometimes being a member of a family isn't about being wrong or right, justified or not, but being there when they need you. Although Janie can't see it right now, she needs you as much as you need her. You're sisters. Family."

The alert on her phone went off. "I'm sorry, but my ride is here. It was nice meeting you, Lenore."

"You, too, Anna. Perhaps, sometime in the future, you might be willing to share a meal with an old woman? Next time I get into the city?"

"Of course." Anna studied the woman. "I'd give you my number but something tells me you already have it."

At the slight nod, Anna knew she'd guessed right.

She clutched her carry-on and pulled it behind her as she followed the walkway past the gate and pushed through the reporters who threw their questions until the moment she slid onto the backseat of the car.

She didn't look back as they drove away.

NICK STOOD at the window in Malcolm's office, watching as Anna pushed through the reporters outside and climbed into a sedan. His heart was heavy as he watched the car slowly move away down the road until he couldn't see it anymore.

She'd left. Like any guilty person who set the fuse to blow the place before making an escape.

From behind him, Dax was still pleading with Janie to listen to him, something that he'd been doing for almost five minutes. Nick was only here now to act as an arbiter of sorts even though he'd have preferred to be anywhere else.

"I can't look at you right now," Janie said, her fury still evident. "Not when it's obvious to me and everyone else that everything that's come out of your mouth has been a lie."

All right. Nick had had enough. These two people loved each other and the sooner they saw that, the better everyone would be. And he could slip away somewhere quiet to think.

"Because you love each other and you're scheduled to say I do to each other in four hours," Nick said, turning to face them, "and unless you're ready for me to go out there and tell everyone—your friends, your family, the minister, the caterers—that you're not going to get married to each other after all, then you need to find a way to work this out."

"Maybe we should call it off," Janie said. "How can I get married to someone I don't even know?"

"That's not true," Dax said, unable to remain quiet. "You know everything you need to know about me."

"Oh, really? Then how come I didn't know you were capable of screwing my best friend moments after kissing me good night? After telling me how happy you were to have me back in your life and that it was fate?"

Dax crossed the room and took a seat next to Janie. "It was fate, and I was glad to have you back in my life."

"Then why did you do it? Why did you sleep with her?" she pleaded.

Dax dropped his head to his hands, his misery evident. "I don't know. Because I was stupid and selfish and not ready for the perfect thing staring right at me. That moment, seeing you out on the beach again, was like a miracle. But when I caught sight of Sara, all this guilt hit me. I owed her an explanation, which was why I met with her later that first night. Before I knew it, we were waking up together, which only confused everything and I needed some time to get my head on straight. So we kept the secret. Hoping to figure things out, but then I got sucked into a pattern and, I'll admit, I was feeling such a high, having two gorgeous women into me." Done with the worst of the confession, Dax raised his head to plead with Janie. "I promise, the minute we got back, I knew who I wanted to build a future with. Who I was meant to be with. You. And I've been terrified of losing you ever since. That's the only reason I didn't tell you."

Nick stepped back, making himself as invisible as he could in the room. They were talking; that was good. The stark pain on their faces spoke volumes about their love and he knew that whatever penance Dax had to pay, they would be okay. Turning, he opened the door and slipped out into the hall.

He needed a breath himself, having felt stuck in the middle of this mire since his mother first appeared at his door. Now, in the dark silence of the hallway, his back leaning against the wall, he closed his eyes and contemplated everything that had happened.

And everything he'd lost in the space of time it took to read a simple five-paragraph story.

He slammed his hand against the wall. Damn. Why couldn't Anna just give him the space he needed? The space he required to process things and come to a solution after weighing all the facts and evidence?

The look on her face when he couldn't tell her what she needed had crushed him.

But at the same time, something held him back from swallowing her denial and moving on. He'd experienced denial before with all the others in his life. Denial was always followed by the bruising, inevitable truth that he'd been used.

Even if he wanted to comfort her, to tell her he was willing to believe her, it was too late now. She was gone. Probably halfway back to the city by now.

She'd left. Run away. Hadn't even tried to fight for herself.

He could think of one reason. Because she had no excuse. No defense. Just like all the others. He didn't know how long he stood there, the grief and disappointment washing over him in waves, when the crashing of something from the other room brought him upright.

A second later, Janie flew out.

Wow. He was worse at judging people than he thought. With a heavy heart, he went inside to check on his brother.

CHAPTER 18

THE SMOOTH, velvety texture of the latte that would bolster her spirits wasn't working its usual magic as she and Tessa sat in the large but homey kitchen at the Montenegros' farmhouse nearly an hour after she'd run away from everything she'd come to love.

If anything, the extra dose of caffeine was making her more jittery and anxious as she remembered the last moments at the Van Hollinses', the looks of anger, outrage, and even disappointment.

"I'm sorry I wasn't there," Tessa said. "Anyone who knows you would know you weren't capable of that kind of deceit."

Rowan Montenegro, the youngest of Tessa's five brothers, waltzed into the kitchen. "You need us to go knock a few heads together, Anna?" he asked, clearly overhearing the tail end of Tessa's comment. He headed to the fridge and pulled out a couple of beers.

"No, but thanks for the offer. Besides, I don't care what they think of me. I know the truth and, like Tessa said, the people who know me know the truth. That's all that matters."

Big words. If only she could force herself to believe them.

It was the kind of posturing she usually took growing up, when she tried to convince herself that she didn't care about the father who had abandoned her or the family that never took the time to get to know her. She didn't need them.

Only, these past few days, having been accepted and welcomed by those same people, she was seeing how different things could be. How it felt to be a part of something. Feeling the love and affection that had come from Janie and Lenore, both of whom had accepted her whole-heartedly just because they were blood, had been...nice.

"All right. But say the word and I can go there right now and set the record straight," Rowan said and flashed her his heartbreaker grin before moseying back out.

Good thing the guy was a totally unapologetic player or Anna might have been in trouble, with all the Montenegro brothers. Dark-haired gods thanks to their Irish mother, and perfect sun-kissed complexion thanks to their Portuguese father, they were stunning, every one of them. Tessa's own complexion was more Irish cream, and with her chin-length raven-black hair, she was like a real-life Snow White. All she needed was a blue bird singing on her shoulder for the image to be complete.

Anna met Tessa's gaze again, noting her friend didn't look any more convinced than Anna by her words. She didn't say anything immediately, instead getting up and grabbing the teakettle from the stove and refilling her mug with hot water and another tea bag. Tessa had always been the more sensitive of Anna's two roommates, the peacemaker who hated conflict, probably in part due to the fact she'd grown up the only girl with five older brothers. Brooking peace agreements had been a matter of survival. It was probably why she'd gone to law school, like their other roommate, Quinn. But whereas Quinn was no-nonsense, practical to a fault, Tessa was the empath, her emotions often getting the better of her.

"Don't look at me like that," Anna said and laughed. "I'm going to be fine. I promise. Charlie has the story that she needed and that has, at least temporarily, gotten me off the hook and kept my job safe. As I see it, I'm no worse off than when this all started."

"If you say so." Tessa looked at her phone. "That's Quinn calling now."

"You didn't tell her about this, did you?" Anna asked in alarm. This was supposed to be a romantic weekend away for her friend. The last thing she needed was to be caught up in Anna's grief.

Instead of answering right away, Tessa walked to the back door and opened it. She turned around, smiling unapologetically as Quinn stood at the threshold. "Of course I did."

"Quinn. You didn't have to come."

"Of course I had to come," she said and swept in, all long legs and graceful motions, her long chestnut hair smooth and silky as it cascaded down her back, her light brown eyes scanning Anna from head to foot as if she were using some x-ray powers to find scars—visible and otherwise. "What good it is having a millionaire boyfriend with his own private plane if you can't take advantage of those perks once in a while?"

It was then that she saw it. With the sun pouring into the kitchen from the open door, causing the facets of the diamond to sparkle, it was hard to miss the ring on her best friend's finger.

Tessa seemed to see it at the same time as she gasped and ran forward, holding the hand up to see the gem better in the light. "You mean he already proposed?" she asked.

"Hmm. From the looks on both of your faces, I'm guessing this isn't coming as a surprise." There was no anger in her words, only pure happiness that seemed to radiate from within. "He surprised me out on the lake this morning. It was...perfect."

As part of the big surprise, James had flown them up to Quinn's hometown in Eureka, Idaho, where he'd hoped to ask her dad's permission before springing the ring on her.

"And you just left all of that? To come and help me?" Anna asked, her throat seeming to close in on her.

"You're darn right, I did. Don't worry, though, James understands. In fact, I think he was relieved to escape from my parents' barrage of wedding-related questions and get back to the city, where we have more privacy. He's outside visiting with Declan and Finn right now."

Though she'd kept the tears at bay for most of the day, seeing the love and concern in her friends' faces, feeling their affection, and knowing that no matter how inconvenient it might have been for them to be there for her caused her to burst into tears again.

In a moment, she was wrapped up in both of their arms.

NEARLY AN HOUR HAD PASSED since Anna's momentary breakdown, and despite the passing of time and the comfort of her friends, she couldn't quite say she was feeling any better. To give Quinn the reassurance she needed before she and James left to finish up their weekend back in the city, she lied and said she did.

As much as her friend wanted to be there for her, some things needed time.

They were outside, walking around the small pond that graced the west end of the Montenegros' property, the warm sun welcome on her swollen eyelids and cheeks. The hummingbirds that dived toward the honeysuckle to her right were another welcome diversion and she watched them battle for one particular succulent bloom.

"She'll be fine," Tessa said, reassuring Quinn as if Anna wasn't right there. "Between my brothers all monkeying for her attention and my excellent nurturing skills, we'll keep her properly distracted until Monday."

Quinn said something else, but Anna didn't hear it, distracted by the buzz of her phone, signaling an incoming text.

Nick.

Her stomach dived, and despite the warmth of the day, she felt cold. Why was he reaching out to her? Did he regret his decision? Or was he going to slay her with more accusations? Taking a breath, she read the message.

Janie is AWOL. Have you heard from her?

Whatever she'd expected to hear, a status update on Janie wasn't it.

"Is everything okay?" Quinn asked, and Anna realized both women were staring at her.

"I...I don't know. It's Nick. Janie's missing."

She hesitated, her fingers over her phone as she decided whether to answer.

Janie was missing. Why should she even care? Janie and everyone else had made it clear that she was persona non grata. They'd professed to like her, maybe even cared about her, but when push came to shove, none of them had her back. None of them had believed in her.

And yet...

There was a lump in her throat as she thought about Janie out there, devastated and alone. Okay, so maybe she cared a little more about her sister than she'd let on. Even to herself.

Trying to ignore the name of the person on the other end of the text, she typed:

No, I haven't. When did anyone last see her?

She waited.

Half hour ago. Dax shows the GPS of her phone has her heading north on Route 12, but battery low. Will lose her soon.

"Do you think she'd do anything to hurt herself?" Quinn asked.

"I don't know. I don't think so."

"Well, it's got to be tough on the girl," Tessa said, her voice oozing with sympathy. "To find out that your fiancé had been sleeping with your best friend, and that they'd been lying about it for years. Not to mention that—right or wrong—she thinks her newly found sister was pretending to like her and then sold her out to further said sister's career."

Anna's moral outrage and crushing disappointment that had fueled her for most of the morning slipped a little. For the first time, she saw things from someone else's perspective.

Yes, Janie had believed the worst in her, but in light of the overwhelming flow of bad news she'd been bombarded with, could she blame her for doubting Anna? Especially considering she hadn't been completely up-front with her from the start.

Instead of being there for Janie during her lowest

moment, wanted or not, she'd run, just like Lenore had said. She hadn't found the courage to stay and fight.

Janie deserved better, and whatever might happen in the next few hours or days or months, even if Janie never forgave her, Anna would never forgive herself if she didn't do something more to help Janie find her happily ever after.

Nick shot out another text. *Any idea where she's going?*

She gritted her teeth at his curt question. If she was going to be mad at anyone, she could save all her energy on this guy, the one who'd made the deal to begin with. He'd made her think that maybe he wasn't a total self-righteous prig but someone with depth and character. He had also convinced her that he was ready to put the past in the past and move on to something that might have been damn spectacular. It had *been* pretty spectacular, even if it was short-lived. But he'd been willing to believe the worst things about her.

No, Nick St. Claire deserved her wrath and so much more.

Quietly seething, she typed.

I left my crystal ball at home. If I find it, I'll let you know.

She slipped the phone back in her pocket and began walking briskly toward the house, Tessa and Quinn following. "I have to find her."

"Of course, and we'll help. Do you have any ideas where she might have gone?"

How the heck would she know? She barely knew Janie. There was a lot she still had to learn, and Anna knew that she wouldn't take no for an answer. She'd show Janie through her actions and her perseverance that she was going to be there, as a part of Janie's life, from now on.

Back in the kitchen, she pulled out her phone again and

went to the map app. North on Route 12? Where could she be going? What did she know about her sister?

She'd been an art history major. She liked the color pink and touch football. Though she'd lived with Malcolm here and in his big penthouse in the city as she grew up, she didn't seem to have much of a relationship with him. Her mother liked to take frequent mental health breaks to various spas around the globe, and the only person that she seemed to feel any real affection for was Lenore, who used to take her to lunch in Seattle, visits to the beach, and...

What was it she'd said? About the carousel ride. She'd never felt safer and happier than that day. It had been in Santa Rosa, which...was probably nearly an hour's drive from the estate. North on Route 12.

"What? Do you have some idea where she could be?" Tessa asked.

"I don't know. Maybe." She relayed her conversation with Janie to them.

"That's only about half an hour drive from here," said Quinn,

"Assuming she's even there," Anna said, biting a fingernail as she considered the options. "With the wedding only three hours away, we could waste a lot of time if we headed there to find out we were wrong."

"What other options are there?" Tessa asked. "Not going anywhere?"

Anna knew that as well. "All right. Let's go."

The time for tears was over. Now it was time to get things done. She needed to make sure Janie realized that Dax loved her and that not standing in front of him this evening before God and everyone to say I do would be a monumental mistake.

Almost as monumental as her thinking she and Nick St. Claire ever had a chance.

NICK REMAINED silent as Dax whipped around a corner almost an hour after Anna's last ridiculous text message. With time running out, his brother had been determined to follow Janie's progress in the hopes of catching up with her before the battery died on her phone.

It would happen any second now if the flashing red battery light on the Find Me app was any indication.

"Easy there, Dax," Nick said as Dax barely dodged the curb as he took the next corner. "You want your next visit to the church to be for a wedding—not our funeral."

"I don't understand where she's going."

That made two of them. As they had since the minute they climbed into Dax's too fast and too sporty car so he could chase the woman he loved, Nick's thoughts returned to Anna.

"You know, I don't understand what Anna was thinking," he said, thinking out loud even though Dax's preoccupation probably meant he wasn't listening. "Is she the slightest bit worried about her sister and the pain she's going through? The pain of being betrayed by her fiancé? Her best friend? Sorry," Nick said quickly when Dax scowled at him. "Not to mention the pain and anguish that Janie might be going through at the possibility that this new sister she was just getting to know could have betrayed her so cruelly. After all, if she hadn't done what she was accused of, wouldn't it have made sense to stick around and force Janie to see the truth? She could have tried to make Janie and everyone else see that she hadn't betrayed them. That she hadn't—"

"Nick, who are you kidding?" Dax asked, his tone impatient. "You mean, why didn't she stick around to try and make you see the truth. Why didn't she stay and fight for you and prove she didn't betray you."

Nick was about to fight his brother on the issue when the truth hit him.

His tirade wasn't about Anna abandoning Janie to deal with the grief. It had been about him.

He clenched his jaw and looked out the window. The answer to his question was glaring back at him.

He'd hurt her. She had needed him to believe her when the chips were down and he hadn't been able to. At least not quickly enough.

Because for all the reasons on one side of the line that told him all the things she had to gain by feeding that story to her editor, the one solitary reason on the other was enough to tell him she was innocent.

Her honesty.

She'd always told the truth, painful as it might be. There wasn't a treacherous bone in her body.

Sure, she tried to be tough. She tried to appear as if she didn't care and that things like family and finding people who accepted her weren't important. In fact, she might have even convinced herself of that.

But he'd seen through it. He'd seen through the wisecracks and eye rolling and knew that she was actually a big softie who had more love, sensitivity, and generosity in her heart than all the people combined in that room this morning accusing her of deceit.

She hadn't had a lot of people in her life who were there for her, to stand up for her and to be her voice when she was too vulnerable to have one. No one was there to stand by her side to support her and have her back.

Least of all him.

The anguish in his gut twisted sharply, leaving him disgusted with himself.

For all her faults, Anna was a woman of her word. A woman of integrity, who wouldn't go behind anyone's back in such an underhanded, mean-spirited way.

Hell, if she wanted to take anyone to the mat, she would do it face-to-face, not hiding behind some anonymous staff byline.

She enjoyed a challenge as much as he did, which was why they were so perfectly matched to each other, complementing each other with their differences as much as their similarities.

"How are we doing? Are we any closer to catching up with her?" Dax asked, drawing Nick from his thoughts.

He glanced down at the phone. The blinking on the GPS that represented Janie was no longer moving. Nick looked around, trying to figure out where they were. "Hang a left."

A half a mile and two right turns later, they pulled up next to Janie's car in the parking lot of Howarth Park. Nick was guessing that the phone was locked inside the vehicle while Janie...was nowhere in sight.

"She can't be far. Why don't we split up and see if we can find her," he said to Dax, who was looking more desperate than before.

"Do you think she's okay?"

"I think she will be now that you're here."

At least Nick hoped so.

Because the sooner those two said I do and wrapped up this day, the sooner he could track down Anna and beg her to forgive him for not being quick enough to see the truth.

CHAPTER 19

ANNA and her friends stood in front of the carousel, their eyes peeled for Janie among the crowd of kids and parents waiting in line to ride on the whirling horses or on the train behind it, or just getting an ice cream from the snack bar.

"I'm not seeing her," Anna said a few minutes later, trying not to let the disappointment overwhelm her. She'd been so sure.

"Well, there are a lots of things here she might be taking in, like the view of the lake, or the hiking trail. Maybe the—"

"Wait." It took another minute before the carousel made it around again for Anna to be sure. When she saw the tear-stained face, the messy blonde hair, and look of hopeless-ness, she knew she'd found her. Anna pointed to her sister. "I've got it from here, guys."

"Okay. We're going to go walk around for a bit. Text us when you're ready."

Anna waited for her sister to exit the ride.

Janie saw her as she reached the gate, her back stiffening.

"I have nothing to say to you," she said and sailed out, returning to the line to get on again.

"That's okay. Maybe you can hear me out," Anna said, following behind her. The entrance gate closed, which meant that the ride was full and she would have the time it took for the ride to finish to talk. "Janie, I know you have no reason to believe me, but I really am sorry."

"Sorry for what exactly?" Janie asked, not turning around.

"Let me go back a step first. I discovered who my dad was when I was thirteen years old. When I looked him up, trying to find out anything I could about him, I found...you. The picture was of the two of you on your eighth birthday and his arms were around you. It broke my heart because... because I wanted to be that little girl. Although I knew it wasn't your fault that Malcolm wasn't part of my life, I did resent you. A lot. So unlike you, on his death, I wasn't surprised to find out I had a sister."

Janie glanced back at her, briefly, as if contemplating what Anna had said. She was listening.

"When you reached out to me, I had no intention of responding. My editor saw the story about Malcolm and his long-lost daughter and threatened me." Anna relayed her editor's ultimatum, leading up to the point when Nick offered her the bargain. "I'm not proud of this, but it is what it is. What I didn't expect was to find out how much I needed a sister and how much I would come to love that sister."

That did it, and Janie turned around to face Anna, tears glistening in her eyes as she nodded. "I never expected to love you as much either," Janie said, holding her hand out.

Anna stared at it for a second before taking it in hers. "I want you to know that that's the extent of my pretense. Yes, I did find out yesterday about Dax and Sara, but I didn't think it was my place to tell you, especially since I knew he'd been wrestling with his guilt for so long and planned on coming clean to you himself. I kept it to myself, temporarily, but I would never have let you walk down that aisle without knowing, even if I had to be the one to tell you. Believe me when I say I would never have humiliated you the way that story did today."

Janie nodded. "I know that. Now. And I'm sorry that I doubted you for a minute. We're sisters. I would have come around eventually, you know," she said, smiling for the first time. "But...how did you know where to find me?"

Anna breathed out a shaky sigh of relief. Half the weight on her shoulders seemed to lift. "You told me all about this place, remember? It was kind of a long shot, but Dax used the GPS coordinates from your phone to estimate the direction you were going. I figured it out from there."

Janie bit her bottom lip. "Have you heard from him? From Dax?"

Now Anna smiled. "You don't seem that surprised that he was spying on you."

She looked a bit sheepish. "It might have crossed my mind that he could find me that way. I guess it was a test to see if he'd come for me." She grew pensive. "But he's not here."

"I'm sure that, once he catches up, he will be. Up until a few days ago, I didn't know that much about Dax other than that he was Nick's kid brother. But in the time I've spent with you both, I can see he loves you and would do anything for you. I also think I can understand, just a little, why he was afraid to tell you. He didn't want to lose you."

"She's got that right."

Anna whirled around, stunned when she spotted Dax

standing a few feet away. Along with Nick. A rush of conflicting emotions hit her at seeing his familiar handsome face.

Hurt. Disappointment. Anger. And yes, even a second of happiness, which was ridiculous.

How long had they been standing there? Listening to her spill her heart out? This man walked away from her, believing the worst things about her, after all the time they'd spent together. He had convinced her that he might be the one person who understood her the most.

She'd been so off base.

Her guard up, she stepped back, allowing Dax to step in between her and Janie.

"Janie. You have to know that you're the only woman on this earth that I want to be with and to see walk down that aisle and promise to love me forever. I screwed up and I will spend the rest of my life making up for that if you can forgive me."

Anna walked a few more feet away, wanting to give them the space they needed to talk. It took her a second to realize that she wasn't alone. Nick was next to her.

"Anna."

She didn't stop, continuing to walk. Nothing he could say would take away the pain that he'd caused her when, in that moment, he doubted her.

"I'm glad you found her first," he said, determined to speak to her despite the quick strides she was taking to get away from him. "I won't try to figure out how you did it, but thank you. It went a long way in helping Dax out of this mess."

She seethed. "I didn't do it for you. Or even for Dax. As you already know, the cat's out of the bag. Our deal is off. I'm not trying to win points from you. I did this because I care for Janie."

He didn't say anything at first, just matched her stride for stride. "You're right to be angry. It took the drive out here for me to clear my head and to let go of some of my own baggage. I had to realize that you're not like any of the other people who've hurt me before, who used me for their own reasons."

"Great. I'm happy for you." It still didn't dampen the fire inside her gut as she remembered the humiliation she'd suffered a few hours ago. Remembered the pain of his rejection, and how how easily he'd let her go. "I hope that you've been spared hours of future therapy."

"Anna, can you please stop for one minute so I can talk to you?"

She wanted to say no, but she also realized that the sooner she got this over with, let him say his piece, the sooner she could close this chapter of her life and move on.

Well, as soon and Janie and Dax made up and got married tonight. *Then* she'd close the chapter on her life that might have once had Nick's pages mixed with hers.

Coming to a halt, she tipped her head impatiently. "Fine. What do you want to tell me, Nick?"

He looked serious, his face drawn tight as if in pain. He licked his lips before speaking, something that once would have had her glued to the movement, wondering at the sensations. Not this time.

"I want to tell you how much of an idiot I am. I shouldn't have needed an hour or even a minute to consider everything when you first asked me. I should have known immediately that you could never have done something like that. Hell...maybe I did, deep down, but I'm not used to trusting the people around me. I've been burned by people who I thought had cared about me and I'm not saying this as an excuse, but so you maybe can understand where I was coming from. It took me longer than it should have for me to realize that you aren't like them. You're not only witty and smart, beautiful and funny, but also honest, to a fault sometimes. I failed you when you needed me most, but I'm here to tell you that it won't happen again."

He exhaled, like he'd been holding his breath until he could say the words.

Words that somehow still cut her like a knife. Because it didn't change the fact that when it really counted, Nick hadn't been there. How many more times would he doubt her and question her intentions?

"I'm sorry, Nick. I know that, right now, you probably mean what you said. All of it. But if something came up tomorrow and I was accused of something just as terrible and the facts were just as damning, would you need another moment to consider everything? Or would you take me at my word and know in your heart that I'm not capable of something like that?"

"Anna, I—"

"No. Please, Nick. I mean, who were we kidding? The idea that you and I could have worked out was ludicrous. There are too many obstacles for us to ever work out."

"I don't believe that. Tell me one."

"Your mother, for one. She hates me, a sentiment that I assure you is similarly reciprocated. She'd sooner set herself on fire than see you with someone like me. Someone who doesn't shine in social situations, who usually says the wrong things and pushes when she should step back. I have no important political or social connections, and other than a small inheritance that I have no intention of ever touching, I'm broke."

"Do you think any of that means anything to me?" he asked angrily, the tic in his cheek pulsing, the fire returned in his eyes as he glared at her.

"I don't know, but it should. A man in your position has to think about those kinds of things. Maybe you don't think you will right now, but it will be important one day." She sighed, her heart weary. "I think that this little meltdown today helped me to put things in better perspective. I don't think we're a good match."

"Now who is making judgment calls? Who's willing to believe the worst things about me even though I'm telling you that you're mistaken?"

This was getting them nowhere, except causing more accusations to be flung about. Accusations that wouldn't change the facts. There wasn't going to be a second chance.

"Maybe I am. Look, Nick. I'm not trying to hurt you or pay you back. I'm just being honest. Once this whole wedding is finally behind us and we go our own ways, you'll see in time that I'm right."

He opened his mouth like he was going to argue with her but instead pursed his lips. She tried to read the expressions that flittered across his face, but they were so fleeting.

"Anna!" Janie called.

Nick glanced back at Janie and then to her again. "There's a lot more we need to say to each other but now's not the time. I'm not giving up, Anna. Not by a long shot."

"Then you're wasting your time."

She turned and Janie reached her, pulling Dax along behind her. "You were right. I know that if I don't make this man my husband today, I'll always regret it. So if we want to have any hope of getting our hair in any kind of semblance of a wedding style, we should go now. Maybe you and Nick can drive back and give me and Dax some time to talk."

Wasn't going to happen. She couldn't be stuck in a car with that man again.

"I have a better idea," she said, her tone even. "Let me talk to my friends, let them know that everything's squared away, and then I'll ride shotgun with you while Dax and Nick follow. You need to build up the anticipation of seeing each other again later tonight."

She was relieved to see Dax and Janie agreed with her. Nick was another story, but she didn't have time to worry about that for long as she parted with the group to seek out her friends.

Nick wasn't part of her story anymore. The sooner he accepted that, the better off they'd be.

WITH DAX'S future no longer hanging in the balance, their drive home had taken more of a leisurely feel with Dax barely bumping up to the posted speed limit. By the time they got back, the bride and her maid of honor were already sequestered upstairs for the full beauty treatment—meaning Nick wouldn't get another chance to try and speak to Anna until after the ceremony.

And speak to her he would, even if he had to lock her into a bathroom with him to get her to hear him out. He wasn't giving up on her. He chose her. First and always.

With two more hours to go before the ceremony, Nick and Dax joined the other groomsmen holed up in Malcolm's study, playing a game of pool and enjoying the Scotch whiskey that he and Anna had partaken of the other night. The other guys didn't know the details of what had happened and weren't too concerned with them either. The status quo had resumed; the wedding was on, and that's all that mattered.

"Let's have a drink," he said to Dax, who looked like he could use it, his face back to a pale almost-green hue. "How you holding up, anyway?" he asked, filling the glasses.

"I'm doing fine," he said, taking one of the glasses. "Well, I'm afraid my stomach is going to turn inside out, but I'm excited, too. The better question might be, how are you doing?"

Nick glanced up at his brother and then back to the decanter that he covered and returned to the side table. "I'll be better when this thing is over and some semblance of normalcy returns to our lives."

"Normalcy is overrated. I kind of prefer the roller-coaster ride that comes from being in love. I think you do, too. You do love her, don't you?"

He didn't have to ask who Dax meant, nor did he have to think about it. "Hell yes."

"Then what are you going to do about it?"

Before Nick could respond, the door of the study opened and their mother stood ominously at the threshold. "Gentle-men, I'm sorry to interrupt, but I need a few words with my sons. Would you mind excusing us? Just for a few minutes and then you can return to your excitement."

Nick shared a glance with Dax, who knew that the use of that lolling, calm tone meant that Kathryn St. Claire was in a dangerous mood.

She smiled at Jake, Chris, and Josh as they meandered out, waiting until the door shut for her smile to reverse into a tight frown. "Would one of you like to tell me why that woman is back in this house? Hasn't she caused enough trouble for one day?"

There was only one woman she could be referring to.

Nick slammed his glass back to the sideboard. "Anna is here because she's as much a part of this wedding as anyone. She's Janie's sister, but more than that—and brace yourself for this—she's the woman I love."

Kathryn's mouth opened in disgust. "All you men are alike, thinking with the little head instead of the one you should. You're just like your father. Can't you see that she's only here to do more damage to this family?"

"I'm not here to argue with you, so I'm only going to say this once. Anna is not responsible for that story."

"Well, then who else had the means and access to make it happen?"

"I don't know and right now it's not my priority."

He glanced at Dax, who shrugged and said, "Maybe it was Sara. She'd seen the writing on the wall and knew it was only a matter of time. This way she could appear the victim, maybe earn some sympathy from you."

"But as your brother and I already discussed, Sara stood to lose more than gain from this," Kathryn said condescendingly, picking up her son's drink and taking it with her as she settled onto a chair.

Nick forced himself to take in some breaths. He wouldn't let her rile him up. He had too many other things to be focusing on.

"No. Maybe she's right, Nick," Dax said, his tone suddenly accommodating. "We should look at who had the most to gain. Who were the primary targets? One would assume they were me and Janie. Someone wanted to break us up."

But that was too obvious, in Nick's point of view.

Okay. If they were doing this...he considered the problem from another point of view. "Let's look at the big picture. What was the biggest impact of this story?"

And as soon as he asked it, the solution was obvious.

Dax seemed to be taking a little longer, as he said, "I don't know. Breaking us up? Telling everyone about your plans to run for the state senate? Tarnishing dad's memory?"

Kathryn didn't answer, only smiling like she was humoring them.

"Any common thread?" Nick asked again.

"I guess...us. Our family."

"And we're missing another obvious fallout. When that story broke, everyone immediately concluded that Anna was responsible, including, to some degree, me, leaving Anna to leave in shame and humiliation. Which might have been the end game all along."

Dax turned his head to stare at their mom.

Kathryn groaned, rolling her eyes. "I feel like I'm in a game of Clue. You don't both think I had something to do with this? What would I have to gain except humiliation when everyone read about my late husband's infidelity?"

"Come on. You love that kind of attention, anything to keep you and the St. Claires relevant." Nick shook his head. "And all this time, I thought it was Sara who was feeding the press all that stuff. I should have known that by hinting at an engagement, a future alliance with the DeWinterses, that you were hoping to set things up that you wanted."

"You needed a nudge. I knew that you and Sara were perfect for each other and you needed that push."

Dax looked like he was still recovering. "You really did this, Mother? Why would you risk hurting Janie like that?"

"Dax, let's be honest. It was your actions that hurt Janie. From what I could gather from Sara, you already were going to tell her. How was I to know that you still wouldn't have come clean before the story came out? I assumed she'd already know. But let's not focus on that, since it all turned out and Janie has forgiven you. Now everyone's talking about Nick and this upcoming election."

Nick loved his mother, and yes, he knew that she loved him and Dax, but sometimes she could be really...awful.

"You're forgetting the most important thing in all this. The most important person—at least to me—is Anna. Anna didn't deserve this." He shook his head. "I won't pretend to understand why you find such pleasure in trying to destroy Anna Blake. Was it because she stood up to you, to the St. Claire name, all those years back in high school? Because she survived your attempts to kick her out of school and off the paper? Probably all of the above. Your actions have been petty, cruel, and undeserved. I'm not going to tolerate any more of it, not where Anna's concerned. You had better get on board with the fact that I'm in love with her and I'm going to fight my hardest to win her back. When I do get her back, if you fail to show her the proper respect and kindness she's due, then I'm not going to be able to have you in my life anymore."

Kathryn's usual smug smile was gone, replaced with shock and maybe even a little regret. Nick didn't have time to stand there and wait for an apology that was probably another year in coming, though. He had things to do if he was going to do what he said and convince Anna to give him another chance.

He headed to the door. "Dax, I'm going to need your help."

"As long as I'm standing in the church in one hour and fifty minutes," Dax said, following him out, "I'm all yours."

Nick knew he had a lot to prove to Anna, that he needed to show her the kind of man he could be. The kind of man he could be with her at his side.

He wasn't going anywhere ever again.

CHAPTER 20

SOMEHOW ANNA HAD MANAGED to smile through the wedding, a ceremony as beautiful as it was heartbreaking to watch. She found Nick's gaze on hers more times than not, his face solemn and his eyes soft. Warm. Like he knew a secret that involved her.

She also had miraculously made it through the endless array of wedding photos that were taken first at the church and then later as they arrived back at the Van Hollins estate, which had been transformed into a fairy-tale-like fantasy of twinkle lights, flowers, and music despite the day's earlier chaos.

Now she only had to make it through this damned reception and, worse, that first dance, then she could escape with Tessa, who was going to be here by ten to rescue her.

If only the happy couple would hurry their butts up and get here already.

The reception was set up on the northern border of the Van Hollins estate where it met the vineyard of the adjoining property. From this vantage point, the guests could see the expanse of the Van Hollins home as it rose on the knoll above them. Anna meandered through the guests who, with drinks in hand, were waiting for the bride and groom to join them for the dinner and dancing.

Janie had lucked out, and the large white canopy that had been rented in case the weather took a turn for the worse wasn't going to be needed. Instead, the tables were artfully laid out around a dance floor with lights strewn above them so it made it feel like extra stars looking down on them. Just as Janie had wanted. The band, located on an elevated stage at the head of the arrangement, was playing the typical music you'd expect at a posh event like this. The tune lifted and carried in the cool but fragrant summer air.

Anna was relieved for the wedges she and the other bridesmaids wore that prevented her heels from sinking into the grass, and that Janie hadn't gone overboard with the dress choices for the bridesmaids. All of them were an acceptable color of a pretty fuchsia pink that didn't remind Anna of a liquid antacid, and a flattering length and cut.

"You look a little better than when I last saw you. Still a little downtrodden, but better." It was her aunt Lenore, dressed in a shimmery light blue dress, her silvery-white hair drawn into an elegant chignon. She looked like a fairy godmother, except for the wand. "I'm glad to see you returned."

"Yeah. Me, too. You were right about running away, and fortunately, I saw that before it was too late."

"I knew you'd end up doing the right thing."

"I'm glad you have such faith in me considering you barely know me. Thanks."

"I hope we're still on for lunch when you return to the city. Maybe I could even come out for Thanksgiving. Make a thing of it with you and Janie and Dax, of course. Your mother would be welcome as well."

"I'd like that," Anna said and surprised herself with how much she meant it. "Although my friend Tessa might kill me if I stiff her on our Thanksgiving tradition of staying at her family's farm. But I think I could figure a way to make it work out."

Her aunt's hand rested over hers. "Good. I look forward to it."

The band that had been playing a pretty, if generic, tune cut off and Anna glanced up to see a few new figures had joined the band. One of them, a guy with dark blonde hair that was a little too long, faded jeans, and a guitar took center stage.

No. Way. It couldn't be—

"Good evening, ladies and gentlemen. I'm sorry to interrupt the previously scheduled musical score, but I've been roped into presenting something of a reprise to you and the bride and groom. Courtesy of the best man, my good friend Nick St. Claire."

Anna's head was spinning as she recognized Dylan Charles. *The* Dylan Charles along with who she assumed were the rest of his band. Nick knew him? Why hadn't he said something when she was talking about liking his music in the car the other day? Whatever the reason, she shook her head at the miracle of the star up there, about to serenade her sister on her biggest day.

Despite her fury at Nick, she couldn't help but feel touched by his gesture and wondered at the strings he'd had to pull to make this happen.

"And now, ladies and gentlemen, may I present to you, Mr. and Mrs. Dax and Janie St. Claire."

The couple in question appeared from around the corner, hand-in-hand. When Janie saw who was up on stage, thanks to a little prodding from her new husband, she stopped and opened her mouth in surprise and let out a shriek before continuing onto the dance floor.

A moment later, Dylan Charles and his band strummed the first beats of a sexy, bluesy song from their first album, instead of the canned song the bride and groom had been practicing to. Tears welled up and threatened to spill as Anna watched Janie and Dax dance, their love and adoration for each other obvious to everyone.

Anna was so drawn into the song and watching the couple, she nearly forgot that in another minute or so she and the others were supposed to join them on the floor. She glanced around, finding Trish and Josh, Megan and Jake, and even Sara and Chris watching from the sidelines. It had been tense for a moment when Janie returned to the house and she confronted the woman, but Janie had a big heart and had been able to forgive her friend who actually appeared contrite. Even now, Sara was smiling at Chris as if with renewed interest.

Anna sensed someone reaching her side, and she turned her head to confirm his presence.

Why did men have to look so painfully, knock-the-breath-out-of-you sexy in tuxedos? It had killed her keeping her eyes off him as they stood in the church earlier, but now having him stand so damn close, she was finding it hard to breathe. She ripped her gaze from him and back to the floor.

You can do this. Just a few more minutes and you'll be free.

"You look beautiful, you know," he said far too close to her ear.

She couldn't respond if she wanted to, her mouth so dry. It wasn't as if Nick had been gone from her mind this entire evening. If only he had.

"How did you pull off this surprise?" she asked and nodded to the stage.

"Oh, Dylan and I go way back, and fortunately for me, he was playing on tour in LA, which made flying him here that much easier."

"Janie loves it."

"And you?"

She shrugged. "It's nice."

"Nice? Well, I was hoping for a bigger reaction than nice." He was teasing her, and she could hear the smile in his voice.

The music kicked up and Anna knew it was time for them to get out there. Not seeing any choice, she took his hand—warm and strong and just as solid as she remembered—and followed him out to the dance floor. She looked at the spot above Nick's shoulder as she waited for that note that would begin their last dance.

And then they were dancing. Swinging and swishing around, so in sync with the other, and for a moment, she felt that excitement in her belly as he swirled her around, looking at her in a way that almost made her believe he cared about her.

Focus. Dance. Don't make eye contact.

Minutes later, her breath coming in choppy gasps, it was over. They all stood and faced the applause. She'd done it. She'd made it through the wedding, the dance, the seeing and touching Nick again. And now she could go.

As she slipped her hand from his, the wrenching it caused her heart made it the hardest thing she'd done.

But it was over, and the sooner she got away and found a corner to hide in, the sooner she'd be able to move on.

THE MOMENT the song had ended, Nick could feel Anna pull

away from him, and not just physically. It was like a rift pushed up between them the moment she let go of his hand.

He needed her to hold on for one more second and give him one more chance—

"I've known the St. Claire boys for some years," Dylan said at precisely the moment Nick needed him to, "and I can see that Dax and Janie are going to have a lively, fun-filled, and happy life together, keeping everyone on their toes" This earned a rouse of applause from the audience. "Now, at the groom's special request, he'd like everyone to feel free to join in the dancing for this next song, one that he wanted to dedicate not only to his lovely bride, but also to the best man and the maid of honor, both of whom I've been assured are a big part of why we're all standing here tonight."

Nick watched the emotions as they ran across Anna's face, first curiosity, then apprehension as she realized what Dylan was asking and, finally, horror as she looked back at Nick.

No escape.

He would have smiled in relief if he hadn't thought it would push her to leave, despite Janie and Dax's request.

He held his hand out to her again. "Come on, Anna. Dance with me? One more time?"

The opening notes streamed out and he watched her face freeze in surprise. "How did you—"

She was wondering how he knew this was her favorite song. Call it a little birdie in the form of a helpful roommate named Quinn who had reluctantly taken his call earlier this evening when he was setting his plan in motion.

He didn't hesitate when her hand slipped back in his, soft and warm, and he placed his other hand around her waist. He inhaled the intoxicating scent that was all hers as she moved along with him to the beat, no longer stumbling as she had that first dance, but boldly and with confidence. She felt right being in his arms.

The sun had slipped fully behind the hills, leaving what felt like just the twinkly lights above them, and he gazed up for a moment at the sight, knowing that he still had a lot of talking to do before he could fully enjoy the beauty around him.

"Anna, I know that you still don't believe me. You still think I'm going to run out on you. But if it takes me appearing on your doorstep with a giant boombox over my head every day and every night for the next ten years to convince you I'm not going anywhere, then that's what I'm prepared to do. I messed up. In that brief moment this morning, I floundered. I can say that from the moment I saw you pulling away from the curb, I regretted my indecision. It nearly killed me to know that the best thing that had happened to me was driving away, possibly forever."

He still got caught up remembering that pain, when everything had felt so dark and lost. Yet here she was, and he had another chance to get it right.

"Anna, you're the one person who's come in and out of my life who has ever truly intrigued me, challenged me, and pissed me off. In the space of the past few hours, I've come to realize that my life only has any real purpose when you're in it. I know we have a lot to learn about each other, a lot to still figure out, but we have time. A lot of time. As long as we're honest with each other and don't hold back, I know we have a chance to have something truly magical. But I need you to give us another chance. I need you to forgive me. Because even though our time has been brief, I know that you're the woman I'm meant to love. Meant to dance with for the rest of my life. Meant to laugh with and enjoy the challenges of every day with, because I will choose you first, Anna Blake. Always."

A tear slipped down her cheek, and he couldn't help but reach out to brush it away, rubbing the warm wetness between his fingers, just as he had last night before.

"Nick. I—" She stopped, too choked up, and he stared into the blueness of her eyes that were luminous and bright like the lightest shades of topaz.

She closed her eyes then, as if closing off his access to her mind, her soul. It felt so final.

Fear took hold of him that what he'd said, what he'd done, was still not enough.

He'd truly lost her.

THE HIGHS and lows of this day had nearly floored Anna more than once, but this moment now...with Nick telling her everything that she could have hoped to hear, whispering every assurance in that low, gruff way of his that had her knees wanting to buckle...

She was flying.

The dark desperation that had hovered over her had shattered, the pieces blown away with every word he uttered. Leaving only this light, blissful, and joyful feeling that made her believe this could be real.

She took in a breath, finding her chest shuddering from the relief and hope she was trying to find her own words to express. She was supposed to be the writer, the person who had a way with words, and here she was. Speechless.

Anna opened her eyes, telling herself not to get lost in the depths of those dark brown eyes before she'd said what she needed to say. "I have my own apologies to make. I shouldn't have run away like I did. You once praised me for my persistence, and I usually am persistent in the other areas of my life, except where it involves my heart. But that's going to change. Because I saw today that my life without you would be like...like trying to dance without a song. Without a tune. You are the music in my head, in my heart, my soul—God, I can't believe I just said that—but it's true," she said and laughed, even through the tears clouding everything in front of her. "What I'm trying to say is that I've fallen hard for you, Nicholas St. Claire. It started ten long years ago and never really stopped."

The wide smile that crossed Nick's face was like a bright, shining light. Then he was crushing her to him, his lips firm yet soft as they touched hers, and it was as if she could feel everything he was feeling. The joy, the relief, the anticipation of tomorrow, as they clung to each other. The strains of the music surrounded them in the air and in their hearts.

Nick leaned back, giving her a chance to catch her breath as she met his gaze again. "I can promise you another thing, Anna Blake. Our life together is going to be colorful, exciting, and—"

"Magical," she said, finishing for him.

"Exactly."

Then he pulled her to him again and she closed her eyes, enjoying the elation and warm-fuzzy satisfaction of finally having her own magical happily ever after.

EPILOGUE

ANNA HUNG UP THE PHONE, trying to keep a poker face as she turned to the expectant gazes waiting around her.

"I'm afraid," she said slowly, watching as the excitement in their faces turned to cautiousness, "that Charlie's going to have to start looking for a new staff writer because...you're looking at the newest staff writer for the *LA Times*."

Her friends' shrieks and cheers were resounding, and she sat back in the crook of Nick's arm and basked in this long-awaited moment. It felt good. No, incredible, made more so because she could celebrate it here with her best friends and the man she had fallen hopelessly in love with two months before.

Finally. The *Times*.

Two months ago, Anna had thought her career was as good as dead when she sat in Charlie's office getting reamed for not exploiting her life for the sake of a story. Little did she know that her career and life weren't over, but they were actually about to begin. She'd not only found a man who loved and adored her almost as much as she did him, and a sister who'd become a permanent and wanted fixture in her life, but after Charlie published her story on Nick the day after she'd run that horrible hit piece on the St. Claires, Anna's career finally had taken off.

With her story becoming one of the most viewed on *The Rundown* for almost a full month—only eclipsed by the story she did on the unexpected elopement of Sara DeWinters to Patriot Linebacker Chris Walker—Anna had the credibility she'd always wanted as a journalist. A journalist who the *Times* was finally interested in hearing what she had to say. And even better, she could continue to work from where she was, submitting her stories to her editor online and making the occasional trips to LA only when necessary.

"This definitely warrants a celebration," Tessa said, returning to their front room with a bottle of champagne tucked under her arm and her hands filled with flutes that James and Quinn took from her.

Anna glanced at Nick, not trying to hide her pride and love. "Not just for me. Early polling shows that Nick is currently more than thirty points ahead of his competitor."

"Go, Nick," Quinn said, a sentiment echoed around the room.

"Wish I could take the credit, but I think a large part of that goes to Janie and her massive base of Instagram followers, who she's tapped into to help drum up support," Nick said modestly.

Anna couldn't argue that Janie had been an unexpected champion to her new brother-in-law's campaign, but she knew that the brunt of his success lay solely on Nick's shoulders for being a candidate people could look up to and believe in.

"Right, honey," she said, patting his knee. "It's entirely Janie." She shared a smile with her two friends. "So you two," she said, turning her attention to Quinn and James, "how is the wedding planning going?"

"Don't ask," Quinn said and groaned. "My parents are set on a wedding back home in Idaho, while James's grandfather insists it has to be here in the city. I think I'm ready to flip a coin."

"Or you could take me up on my suggestion and just do the whole thing in St. Croix," James said.

"And be disowned by both sides of our family? I don't think so," Quinn said, laughing. "I think, other than you, Sabrina would be the only Taylor ecstatic at the chance to scope out St. Croix," Quinn added, referencing her younger sister, Sabrina. "She's always looking for a new location to set her next story."

"Well, you had better decide soon since I'm dying to start planning everything," Tessa said a tad too excitedly.

"You know, Tessa, if you would just take my or Nick's or James's or any of our offers to set you up," Anna said, "you could be planning your very own wedding by the fall."

Tessa groaned. "Right. Kind of like you and Quinn, who shot down every attempt anyone ever made to set you up, including me?"

"She has a point," Quinn said.

"I'll find my guy when the time is right," Tessa said. "And who knows? Maybe I'm destined to be an old maid, the doddering spinster aunt to the dozens of kids my brothers are going to inevitably have."

They laughed again, and Anna sank back into Nick's crook, content at knowing that she had found her partner, her mate, and her friend. Nick seemed to be of the same opinion as he took her hand, tracing his fingertips across its surface until goose bumps ran up her arms.

Hours later, long after Tessa said good night and slipped

away into her room and Quinn and James left to his place, where they usually went every Saturday night after the week wrapped up so they could spend time exclusively with each other, Anna and Nick sat on the couch, still in each other's arms.

It was Anna's favorite time of the day, when they could be alone without the interruption of phone calls or texts from Anna's editor or Nick's campaign or his office where he still did his work as the city supervisor.

"I still can't believe that I'm officially a reporter for the *LA Times*."

"I can. I always knew you were destined for greatness, Anna Blake. Now it's only a matter of time before we'll be celebrating your winning the Pulitzer. I give you another five years, mark my words."

"Shh. You can't say that out loud. You'll jinx it. Besides, it will probably be ten years, at least."

"Ten years does seem to be the magic number around here. God knows it took me ten years to finally get the one thing in my life that has given it any real meaning."

"Oh? That parking space in your condominium?"

He tickled her, and she giggled, holding her hand over her mouth so as not to wake up Tessa.

"And how about you, Mr. City Supervisor? What lofty aspiration do you hope to have achieved in the next ten years? Maybe US senator? Or how about governor?"

He shook his head, his eyes warm and happy as they settled on her. "Everything I could ever want is here in my arms right now."

She should groan about now at his cheesiness. Maybe laugh and offer some wittier response. But it was hard to argue with the truth. Because Pulitzer or no Pulitzer, career at the *Times* or anywhere else, none of that really mattered in the grand scheme of things.

Because the only thing she needed was to have Nick holding her and loving her and reminding her each and every day that he'd not only chosen her but they had chosen each other. And it was all they needed.

Meeting his gaze, she smiled.

"Ditto."

Want to read more from the
CRAZY IN LOVE SERIES?

Grab CRAZY FOR THE ROCK STAR
BOOK 3 of the CRAZY IN LOVE series
from Amazon

WANT TO HEAR ABOUT UPCOMING RELEASES?

Subscribe to my newsletter and stay up to date on the latest releases, cover reveals, and giveaways! Type in the link: http://bit.ly/2cd3SvQ

Love You Madly

Thriller

Deceived

ABOUT THE AUTHOR

Ashlee Mallory is a *USA Today* Bestselling author of sweet romantic comedy, suspense, and thrillers. A recovering attorney, she currently resides in Utah with her husband and two kids. She aspires to one day include running, hiking, and traveling to exotic destinations in her list of things she enjoys, but currently settles for enjoying a good book and a glass of wine from the comfort of her couch.

Ashlee loves to hear from readers. You can find her at any of the following links, so please feel free to drop her a line, or subscribe to her email list and keep updated with any news of upcoming releases, sales, and giveaways by clicking here: Newsletter.

You can also find her on:

Facebook | Twitter | ashleemallory.com | Goodreads